NIGHT CALLS

Other books by Holly Jacobs:

Pickup Lines
Lovehandles

NIGHT CALLS

•

Holly Jacobs

AVALON BOOKS
NEW YORK

Published by Thomas Bouregy & Co., Inc.
160 Madison Avenue, New York, NY 10016

Library of Congress Cataloging-in-Publication Data

Jacobs, Holly, 1963–
    Night calls / Holly Jacobs.
        p. cm.
    ISBN 0-8034-9764-4 (acid-free paper)
    1. Women in radio broadcasting—Fiction. 2. Erie (Pa.)—
Fiction. 3. Talk shows.—Fiction. I. Title.

    PS3610.A35643N54 2006
    813'.6—dc22

                                    2005033846

PRINTED IN THE UNITED STATES OF AMERICA
ON ACID-FREE PAPER
BY HADDON CRAFTSMEN, BLOOMSBURG, PENNSYLVANIA

This one's for Jane, Kevin, Hanni, Liesl, Brigitta and Ameliarose! And a special thanks to Winston, who inspired Cassie's Dudley in the book!

Prologue

"*E*rie, *Pennsylvania, is a little city with a big heart. And the heart is what Night Calls is all about. Come join us here at WLVH for the next four hours. We'll be listening to love songs as we talk about love—how to find it, how to save it, how to treasure it.*

"I'm Cassiopeia Grant here on WLVH's Night Calls—where love is more than just a song. I'm waiting to hear from you, Erie."

Celine Dion's Titanic *theme filled the airwaves.*

When it ended, listeners heard Cassie say, "Hi, this is Cassie and you've reached Night Calls here on WLVH, where love is more than just a song."

"Hi, Cassie. This is Patty. I listen to Night Calls every night."

"Thanks, Patty. We at WLVH appreciate our loyal

1

listeners. So, what do you want to talk about tonight? A man who's done you wrong, or one that's
oh-so right?"

"Neither. I just wanted to wish you the best with
your upcoming marriage."

"Thank you. Like we say here at Night Calls, love
is just a heartbeat away. In my case, it's just a weekend away. I can't tell you how excited I am. Gene and
I will be the third generation from my family to
elope. I only hope our marriage is as happy as my
parent's and grandparent's."

"I'm sure it will be. Sometimes I worry that I'll
never find that kind of love. All the men I date are
losers."

"Listeners of Night Calls know that I've dated
my share of Mr. Wrongs. But you have to believe
that the right man for you is waiting out there. You
just haven't found him yet. You can't give up.
There are a lot of fish in Lake Erie . . . one's bound
to be right for you."

"There are too many fish . . . too many choices.
It's not as if the perfect man is living next door."

"Maybe, maybe not. The idea is to leave yourself
open to the possibility. With love anything is possible. I hope you'll come out to our WLVH Second
Annual Splash Bash. Who knows . . . maybe Mr.
Right will be there waiting. Let's let Cher tell us just
how to know if we've found the right man."

Cassie cued the CD and Cher began to tell her

audience how to tell if a man loves a woman—with a kiss.

Cassiopeia Grant leaned back in her chair and smiled.

Life was perfect.

Chapter One

Perfect, Cassiopeia Grant thought as her neighbor, Jonathan Cooper, stepped over the small hedge that separated their homes.

"Mrs. Gifford," he said with a smile. "Let me be the first to congratulate you."

Coop might say congratulations, but Cassie knew he didn't mean it. He was pretty vocal about his opinion of marriage.

And she knew what he was going to say when she told him what had happened.

What did I tell you? Love is just an official rationalization for forming a partnership, or having sex. Either one is preferable minus the sugarcoating.

"Mrs. Gifford," he repeated, his smile fading

4

when he saw Cassie's expression and he looked concerned. "You're home."

"Yes, I'm home. One might expect a more profound statement from you. After all, anyone could see I'm home. Here I am, standing with my suitcase in my driveway so of course I'm home. Stating the obvious isn't normally your forte. Has anyone ever told you that you aren't the brightest bulb in the socket?"

"I mean," he started with the slightly exasperated tone so many people used with her, "aren't you supposed to be tucked in some romantic honeymoon suite right now?"

A small sniffle tickled her nose.

Cassie ignored it.

She wasn't going to cry again. She was done crying.

Grandma Rose used to say it was no use crying over spilled milk, and she'd probably add, *or failed weddings.*

No, Cassie was all done crying. Just because she was the first person in three generations of Grants to almost sell out and marry for less than true and everlasting love, just because she'd almost made the biggest mistake of her life, just because she didn't get her walk down the aisle, that didn't mean she had to cry about it. It was over.

Over.

Like all her hopes for a marriage like her parents had. A marriage like her grandparents had had. Like all her aunts, uncles and cousins had. Over.

No, she wasn't going to cry just because her life felt hopeless and loveless. She'd decided on the trip home that she was going to be a career woman. Yes, she was going dedicate herself to her job and forget about finding true love.

And she wasn't going to stand here and sniffle because she was the lone Grant who couldn't find a happily-ever-after. She was starting a new family tradition. Independence.

"Cassie?"

She opened her purse, searching for her keys to her small house.

"Your honeymoon?" Cooper prompted.

Trying to sound dignified rather than on the verge of tears, Cassie said, "It would be hard to have a honeymoon when there wasn't a wedding. I'm old fashioned that way. You see, I'm not Mrs. Gifford, or Mrs. Anything-else. I'm still just plain old Cassiopeia Grant."

She dug to the bottom of her purse but still couldn't find her keys. Thank goodness she'd caught a cab home from the airport and wasn't stuck in the parking lot looking for them.

She'd lost her fiancé and now she'd probably lost her keys as well. If the last twenty-four hours had proved anything, it was that Cassie was very good at losing things, from keys to grooms.

"Want to talk about it?" Cooper asked.

"No." The word came out hard and brisk, and

Cassie instantly felt bad. This entire mess wasn't Cooper's fault.

She smiled, hoping to soften her harsh tone. "I don't think I'm quite ready to talk about it yet. Sorry if I'm being a bit testy."

"If I can't make you feel better by offering an ear, than I have two other options."

Cassie stopped her futile search for her keys a moment and glanced at Cooper. "Such as?"

"One, I could offer you my shoulder and you could cry all over it." He didn't look exactly thrilled at the prospect.

"Knowing how much men enjoy bawling women, I'll thank you for the gallant offer, but I'll decline. I'm not going to cry about Gene Gifford or unrealized dreams. I'm going to pick myself up and move on."

A look of intense relief swept over Cooper's perfectly chiseled face.

Her neighbor was a hunk. No doubt about it. Not that Cassie had ever noticed. No. She knew too much about Cooper to let a little thing like heart-rattling good looks influence her opinion.

After all, tall dark and handsome had to be weighed against his rather pessimistic worldview. Grandma Rose used to say, "Pretty is as pretty does."

Jonathan pretty much did everything opposite to the way Cassie did.

Oh, he made a good friend, but would never be anything more. Jonathan Cooper didn't believe in love and although Cassie had decided that she didn't believe in it for herself anymore, she couldn't afford to not believe in it for other people.

Love was her livelihood. If nothing else, she'd have to at least go through the motions, because as of her aborted wedding, she was a confirmed career woman. A Mary Tyler Moore of the new millennium.

"Well, then, if you don't want to cry, maybe you'd prefer I go find good old Gene and bash him one."

"Now, that sounds more like the Jonathan Cooper I've grown to know so well these last few months. With all those violent tendencies of yours, I can't imagine how you ended up a lawyer. I mean, people are coming to you solve their problems? Someone like you tends to cause them." She grinned, which she knew had been his intent.

Cooper—he wouldn't let anyone call him by his given name and she'd learned to even think of him as Cooper—who liked to pretend he was tough, but was really soft like a marshmallow. A dinner-mooching marshmallow who'd turned out to be a very good friend.

Cassie went back to sifting through her purse's contents, looking for her elusive keys. Aspirin, bandages, sunscreen.

No keys.

Date book. Pens, lots of pens. Change rattled around the bottom of the purse.

Hey, there was the pack of carmels she'd thought

she'd lost. She opened the wrapper of one and popped it in her mouth as she continued hunting and smiled.

Life might fall apart, but good carmel was good carmel.

"Does that little smile mean you're imagining how fun it would be if I smashed good old Gene right in the face?"

The incongruity of suave, sophisticated Jonathan Cooper smashing anyone made Cassie more than smile, she laughed.

"How can I wallow in self-pity if you're hanging around cheering me up?"

Eureka. She managed to snag her key chain, hiding behind the zippered makeup pouch she carried.

Cooper shrugged. "I guess you don't get to wallow at all today."

Grateful that she'd managed to find her keys, even if she hadn't managed to locate her groom yesterday, she opened the door. "I suppose you want to come in?"

Cooper's right hand flew to his chest. "My fair lady, such a pretty invitation is next to irresistible."

She left the door open and tossed the suitcase on the couch, followed by her purse.

It was debatable which made the biggest bounce.

She just kept right on walking into the kitchen. "Do you want something to drink? There's soda or ice water."

"I'll take a soda if you'll talk to me."

Obviously feeling at home, Cooper helped himself to a seat at the kitchen table.

Cassie dug through the refrigerator and pulled out two cans of cola. She tossed one to him, popped the tab on the second one and took the chair opposite him. "So, what do we talk about? Did something exciting happen in the neighborhood while I was gone?"

"You just left yesterday," Cooper pointed out.

"Thanks for reminding me." She'd left Friday morning full of high hopes . . . and here it was Saturday afternoon and she had no hope at all.

No hope of ever finding love.

"Talk to me, Cassie," Cooper said softly. "We're neighbors, remember?"

She offered him what she knew was a weak smile. "And if you can't talk to your neighbor, who can you talk to?"

"Sometimes it's easier to talk to someone who has no vested interest." He reached across the table and took her hand. "What happened in New York? You had the license, you had the groom, you were all ready to elope. But . . . ?"

"But I realized that Gene and I . . . well, it was a mistake. I might actually have gone through with the wedding if I'd arrived on time. But he booked some cut-rate flight that was supposed to take me from Erie to Pittsburgh to Chicago to New York."

"Why backtrack to Chicago?"

"It was cheaper. But the airline threw an extra leg into the mix, and I ended up in Orlando with a six-hour layover, which turned into an overnight layover because of some engine problems. And all that time by myself forced me to think, because rather than worrying about missing my wedding, I felt . . . relieved. I realized I want romance and true love, not settling for what I had with Gene. I realized I don't truly love Gene, I just liked the idea of loving him."

"Now, hang on a minute, just because you got cold feet, doesn't mean you don't love him."

She shook her head. "It was more than cold feet. On that long, long flight I discovered something. I never loved Gene in an all-encompassing, till-death-do-us-part kind of way. And he deserves that—everyone deserves that, even me. Since Gene took my returning his ring with such accountant-like calmness, I can only assume he never loved me that way either."

"Honey, Gene takes everything with calmness. He might as well have been a calculator as an accountant—it always seemed to me he showed about as much emotion."

"You didn't like him?" Cassie was surprised to hear Cooper say that. After all, everyone liked Gene.

"I didn't like Gene *for you*," Cooper clarified.

"Why didn't you say something? You're supposed to be my friend."

"Gene was around long before I was, and you said you loved him. You were engaged to him before I ever moved in next door, and I didn't think it was my place to say anything, so I let it go."

"Let it go? Let it go?" Cassie felt hysteria mounting. Deliberately, she tried to speak calmly and lowered her voice as she asked, "That's what friends do, Cooper? They just let things go?"

"Come on, Cassie, what's really eating you?"

"What's eating me is I'm a twenty-nine-year-old host of Night Calls . . . a radio show that's devoted to love. My business is love. I'm supposedly an expert. People call me with their problems." She slammed her pop can down and a small amount dribbled onto the table.

"But my problem is I can't find real love for myself. It's old fashioned, I know, but what I want is to find someone to love and commit to. Someone who will love me in return. I want a man who wants kids, carpools, the whole works. Is that asking too much?"

"No." Cooper paused a moment. "You'll find that someone eventually. It just wasn't Gene Gifford."

"And it wasn't Martin Freid, or Stu what's-his-name, or—I'm beginning to suspect it's not anyone. I'm destined to spend my life finding someone for everyone but me."

"Maybe you're trying too hard. Relax." Cooper paused a moment, as if he was searching for something to say. "They say love happens in its own time."

"*They say,* but you don't, right?"

Jonathan Cooper was the most antilove person she knew. Antilove, anticommitment. She knew his views on the subject.

"We've had this debate before, Cassie. I don't think you're up for another round in your present condition."

"You're wrong. I don't think I'm going to debate the issue of love with you anymore, at least not where I'm concerned. I'm done with love, with men. You know how they say, today is the first day of the rest of your life? Well, it is. I'm going to make some changes. Big changes. The first of which is I'm done looking for love."

"What about your show?"

"No. I might be questioning love, but the show's my life. The rest of my family has found lifetime sort of loves, so it does happen. Even if I'm feeling cynical about it at the moment and know I'm destined to be a spinster, I'm not totally writing love off, at least not for others. Just for me."

She was done with searching for love for herself. The thought should comfort her, after all there was obviously no perfect match for her. But rather than being comforting, the thought just left her feeling . . . hollow.

She eyed her neighbor. "Let's change the subject. How did your date go with Kristy last night?"

Finding a woman for Cooper had become her pet project, maybe she had got that right.

"I wish I could tell you we're an item, but—"

But. There seemed to be a lot of buts in her life lately. Cassie was beginning to feel as if she was the *butt* of some cosmic joke.

She took a healthy gulp of her soda and sighed. "*But* I failed once again."

"Not failed. You told me up front you didn't feel we were right for each other, but you didn't think a date would hurt. And it didn't. It was just, well, I don't think Kristy and I were destined for any great romance."

Better to face the music right up front, rather than avoid it. "What was wrong with her?"

"It seems like a petty annoyance, but . . . well, she flossed."

"She flossed, as in she flossed her teeth?"

Cooper nodded, confusing Cassie even more.

"You find dental hygiene a petty annoyance?" she asked, unclear what flossing and dating had to do with one another.

Cooper shook his head. Not one of his perfect dark strands of hair fell out of place. "No. But I find talking about it at the table gross. Do you know she carries floss, a toothbrush, and toothpaste with her? And not just for emergencies."

"Really? She's that much of a stickler that she can't wait until she gets home to brush?"

"Apparently not." He gave a small snort of disgust. "She said she'd paid a fortune for her smile and wasn't about to take a chance messing it up with poor dental hygiene."

"Hmm, you know . . . yes, they could be perfect for each other."

"Who's perfect?"

"Kristy and Terry. He's my—"

Cooper cut her off. "Your dentist?"

"You got it. I'm sure he'll find Kristy's oral diligence appealing."

"And just think, she can have a professional cleaning any time she wants it."

"Terry and Kristy," she murmured. "They're perfect."

"Cassie, your so-called cynicism lasted a record five minutes. Admit it, you're a hopeless romantic. You can't give up on love just because Gene Gifford wasn't the man for you."

She sighed. "Like I said, I'm not. At least not for others. But me? I'm just resigning myself to being an eccentric spinster who relieves her own sexual frustration by helping others find true love. Love is my job, and I'm going to treat it as such; as a career, not a personal aspiration."

"Don't you think that will be a little lonely?" Cooper asked.

"I'll find companionship the way all spinsters have always found companionship."

"A cat?" Cooper asked with a smile.

Cassie didn't answer. She just smiled back at him, relieved that she had a plan for life. A career and a pet.

Yes, that would do just fine.

Monday morning, Cassie went to WLVH and knocked on the door of Craig Warner, the new station manager.

"Come in," he barked through the door.

Craig was good at barking.

Before working at the station he'd been a sergeant in the Marine Corps so barking was second nature.

He still had the look of a soldier. Short gray hair, ramrod straight posture, and a tendency to give orders rather than make requests. But once you chipped through the tough-guy facade, there was a man with a heart of gold.

He looked concerned as she walked into his office. "Cassie? What are you doing back? You had the week off."

"Not anymore. I want to come back to work tonight," she said as she took a seat. "I need to come back."

"What happened?" Craig asked.

"The question is, what didn't happen. The answer is, the wedding. I didn't marry Gene."

"He got cold feet?"

There was a look in Craig's eye that didn't bode well for Gene's feet or any other body part.

"No," she said hastily. "Gene didn't. I did. Well, not actually cold feet. I realized I never loved him the way I should have, so I called it off. I got back Saturday and I'm already going stir crazy. I need to come back to work. I know you were going to do a week of 'The Best Ofs,' but please?"

"You're sure you're okay?"

"As okay as I can be. Work will help."

"You know we'd rather have you on the air than just repeats. Better for the ratings." Under his breath he added, "And we need all the ratings we can get."

"Great," she said, relieved to know she had something to do other than sit at home and mope. "I'll be here tonight. I've got things to do today."

He looked at her suspiciously. "You've got a look in your eye. What's up?"

"Well, since I've decided that I'm destined for singleness, I'm getting—"

"A cat?" he asked, repeating Cooper's question with a hint of laughter in his voice.

"You're the second person to ask that. It would be rather stereotypical, don't you think? Plus," she added with a grin, "I'm allergic. I'm getting dog."

"You know how you're always talking about destiny? Just so happens, Levi's definitely taking the job in California and moving in with Celeste. Her apartment doesn't allow dogs, so he's looking for a home for his."

"Really?" Cassie felt a spurt of happiness. Celeste and Levi. That was good.

And he had a dog that needed a home?

"I want a big dog, not some chihuahua," she said. "It will take a big dog to help me forget what a mess I almost made of my life. Marrying a man I didn't really love just because I wanted to be in love."

Craig laughed. "Honey, this truly is destiny. Levi's dog is just a puppy, but there's no doubt about the fact he'll be a big dog. Big enough to make you forget just about anything."

Craig looked uncharacteristically happy.

"Is there something you're not telling me?" she asked.

"Nothing. Like I said, this dog is just what you ordered."

Still not convinced there wasn't something going on, she asked, "Can I use your phone?"

"Help yourself," Craig said still smiling.

Craig didn't smile often. He tended to sport a military sort of scowl most of the time. The fact that he was smiling didn't bode well.

"There's nothing wrong with the dog, is there?"

"Cassie, if you can't trust your boss, who can you trust? Call Levi and go see it for yourself. You decide."

Cassie dialed Levi's number. Here was an instance

where her matchmaking paid off big time. She had no doubts Levi and Celeste would be happy.

Maybe Levi's dog would return the favor and make Cassie happy in return.

She hoped so.

Chapter Two

"This is Night Calls on WLVH, where love is more than just a song."

"Hi, Cassie, this is Charlie. My girlfriend claims that I don't have a romantic bone in my body."

"Do you?" Cassie asked.

Charlie sighed. "Probably not. But I want to do something special for her for her birthday. Any suggestions?"

"That's a great topic for tonight's show. Ladies, do you have any suggestions on how Charlie can make this one to remember?"

Cooper stared at the computer screen Monday afternoon. He'd left the office early, hoping to catch up on his paperwork here at home, away from distractions.

Unfortunately, he kept glancing at the small white house across the driveway, unable to get Cassie's sad expression out of his head.

She'd always had such a warped view of marriage and romance.

Love? Who could define it?

Cassie thought she could. Her definition consisted of something that was all flowers and candy, champagne and candlelight.

Romance.

Cooper shook his head and turned off the computer screen. He leaned back in his chair and peered out the window, the window that faced Cassie's house.

Love was a four-letter word.

Despite his neighborhood matchmaker's attempts to find him the love his life, Cooper doubted there was such a person.

He'd seen too many couples who had once been *in love* walk through his office door looking for blood as they tried to release themselves from their vows to love one another forever.

No, Cooper didn't believe he'd ever find the love of his life.

One day he'd find some compatible woman and settle down, but their relationship wouldn't have anything to do with Cassie's mythical love. It would be a partnership. Two people joining together to work toward a common goal. There would be compatibility, friendship even, and maybe those feelings could be interpreted as Cassie's fairy tale love, but Cooper knew better.

Love was just a romantic joke. And just in case he and his someday-partner forgot the punchline, Cooper would see to it that they had their pre-nup signed and dated before saying their I do's.

Cassie was probably better off with a cat than with a man. No man in the world could ever live up to her romantic expectations.

Maybe she'd learned her lesson and would outgrow those views and settle on a nice, practical relationship—the type of relationship Cooper would have someday.

Cassie's small green Volkswagen pulled into the driveway. Cooper watched with a certain sense of appreciation as one leg followed another out the door. They were long legs for such a comparatively tiny lady. Really, with her short blond hair, her petite build, and the blue eyes he knew sparkled under her brows, she looked like a wayward pixie . . . except for those legs.

But as nice as her legs were, it was her eyes that really spoke to him. He'd spent a great deal of time studying them.

They weren't the normal muddy shade of blue, or that sort of grayish, hazel blue. No Cassie's were robin's egg blue—bright and inquisitive. They seemed to say more than most people could say verbally. They reflected whatever she was feeling. Those feelings were there for the world to read, and she didn't seem to mind at all.

Cooper, who guarded his thoughts and feelings, couldn't comprehend Cassie's openness. It bothered him, and yet, he was drawn to it.

How could someone like Cassie not find a man who would at least pretend to believe in love long enough to woo her? Cooper puzzled over Cassie's lack of suitors as she walked to the back of the car and opened the door.

She had probably been shopping. She'd said she had cleaned out her cupboards before she left. And to the best of his knowledge she hadn't left the house all weekend. He'd thought about going over to cheer her up, but had opted to give her some privacy instead.

But it was Monday and she looked as if she was done moping. He should probably be a good neighbor and try to cheer her up and carry the grocery bags in for her.

He glanced at his watch. Almost four. That meant he stood a good chance of Cassie offering him dinner if he was there. And he'd be there if he carried in her shopping.

In the two months he'd lived here, he'd eaten at Cassie's more often than he'd eaten at his own house. Her fiancé had been busy with some major project at his company, and since she was spoken for, there had been none of that tense man-woman thing between them. Just a casual friendship. Cassie might be a bit distracted about some things, but could she ever cook.

Suddenly Cooper stopped fantasizing about Cassie's cooking and concentrated on what she was taking from her car. It wasn't a grocery bag, it was . . .

A monster of a dog. At least he assumed it was a dog.

The beast's head almost reached Cassie's hips. The animal had gold fur covering its body, and no hooves, so it couldn't be a horse.

No, it had to be a dog, but Cooper couldn't remember ever seeing an animal quite like this one.

Dinner was suddenly forgotten as he made his way to Cassie's house.

"What on earth is that?" he hollered.

The beast was still sitting by the car, staring mournfully at Cassie as she tugged at the leash attached to its collar.

Frustration was etched in her face. "It's a dog. What did you think it was?"

"Some mythical beast?" He paused momentarily studying the thing. "A horse, maybe?"

"A dog." She gave another tug. "*My* dog."

"You got a dog? I thought you were getting a cat."

She dropped the leash and whirled around. "I'm allergic to cats, and to be honest, even if I wasn't, I wouldn't want to fall into anyone's idea of a stereotype. So I got a dog."

"You bought this beast on purpose?"

"He's not a beast." She covered the thing's ears and whispered, "Don't say that. You'll hurt his feelings."

She let go of his ears and massaged his massive head. "A big dog like this is bound to have very big, sensitive feelings."

"You still haven't explained why giving up on love and being allergic to cats means you brought this beast, er . . . dog home."

"I haven't given up on love, just on finding *my* love. I told you that. I've decided that I'm going to collect dogs."

"Dogs? As in plural?"

"Yes." She hesitated. "Okay, so maybe more dogs someday, but right now I'm starting with Dudley."

"Dudley?"

"I know," she said with a sigh. "It's not a dignified name, is it? But that's what Levi named him. I'm afraid he's confused enough without me messing with his name, so Dudley he is."

"Why did his previous owner get rid of him?" Cooper asked, though he had no problem imagining why the very intelligent previous owner decided to de-dog their life if Dudley was the dog in question.

It would take a mansion to house this beast comfortably. A mansion or a stable, neither of which Cassie had on hand.

"You know Craig, at the station? Well, Levi is his brother. I introduced him to Celeste earlier in the year at a party. She was an intern at the station. She was dressed like a princess, he was a knight. I knew right then that they were a good fit. Anyway, they've been dating ever since. Celeste just got a job in California, and Levi's going to move in with her. Unfortunately, the apartment doesn't take dogs."

"Still," Cooper said slowly, eyeing the beast, "what do you think you're going to do with something this big?"

"Dudley's perfect for me. The moment I looked at those great big chocolate eyes, I knew he was meant to be mine."

She picked up the leash and gave another tug.

She gave another tug. "Come on, Dudley. We're home."

"Would you like some help?"

"No, that's okay. Dudley just has to get used to me, that's all." Bracing her feet, she pulled harder. "Come on, boy."

Cooper watched the scene, trying to hide his smile. The dog outweighed Cassie. There was no way she was going to budge him if he didn't want to be budged.

"Really, Cassie, let me just get him into the house."

She threw the leash over her left shoulder and turned, pulling on the beast for all she was worth. "I said I've got him."

At that moment, Dudley decided to move, all of half a foot. But half a foot was enough for Cassie to go sprawling on the ground.

"Are you okay?" Cooper asked. Concern warred with amusement, though he tried to mask the latter.

Cassie took his hand and accepted his assistance. "I'm fine. I merely dented my dignity a bit." She glared at Dudley. "Bad dog."

Dudley didn't look a bit sorry. He looked as amused as Cooper felt. "Ready for me to take a turn?"

Cassie nodded. "Be my guest."

Cooper picked up the leash and gave the dog his most authoritative look. "Dudley, come."

The giant dog rose, and Cooper felt smug. "See, it just takes a firm hand."

Dudley walked right up to Cooper, sniffed once, then lifted his leg and let loose onto Cooper.

"Dudley," Cooper roared, his smugness replaced by the warm, wet feeling dripping down his pant legs.

This time all the amusement was Cassie's. "I think I've read that dogs only pee on your legs if they like you. They're sort of marking you as their territory. Dudley must really like you a lot."

"Bad dog," Cooper growled, as he dragged the beast to Cassie's front door. "Could you stop laughing long enough to open this door?"

Between giggles she dug through the monstrous bag she called a purse for her keys. How much stuff did one woman need to lug around with her?

"You know, it might be easier if you clipped the keys onto something," he said.

"Oh, I have a cute little loop on the top of the purse just for that, but I always forget to do it until I can't find my keys, then I wish I had."

"Someday you're going to have to get organized, Cassie."

She shot him a hurt look and Cooper could have kicked himself, except his pant leg was too gross to kick anything.

"Sorry," he muttered. "I'm not feeling very nice at the moment."

"No, I imagine you're feeling quite pissy."

Humor once again reigned supreme. Hearing her laugh was almost worth his wet leg.

Almost.

"Found them," she cried. She unlocked the door and flung it open wide. "This is your new home, Dudley."

Cooper unhooked the leash from the dog's ridiculous rhinestone-studded collar and gave him a little push through the door.

"I don't suppose you want to come in?" Cassie asked.

"I think I'd better head home and shower."

"Yeah, probably. Thanks for the help," she called as he trudged across the lawn and stepped over the hedge into his own yard.

Cooper needed to get a handle on his life. It was crazy.

There had been that dud of a date with floss-her-teeth Kristy. Then his wacky neighbor's missed wedding, and the ever-present threat of female tears. Add to that, he'd been peed on and lost his chance at an edible, free meal.

Jonathan Cooper was definitely feeling a bit pissy.

"You're going to like it here, Dudley," Cassie soothed as the big dog paced to and fro across her kitchen floor.

Dudley's kibble sat in the brand-new stainless steel dog dish untouched. The giant raw-hide bone sat gloriously new and pristine beside it. Dudley hadn't moved beyond her kitchen, but he'd certainly moved through her kitchen.

Back and forth, back and forth.

"Do you want to tell me about it?" she asked sympathetically. But her question didn't help. Dudley wasn't talking.

Back and forth, back and forth.

"You're making me seasick, Dudley."

Cassie sat at the kitchen table watching her dog pace while continuing to talk to him.

Maybe she should be worried. Talking to dogs couldn't be a sign of a healthy mind. It was almost as bad as talking to cats. A very spinsterish thing to do.

If she had any doubts about her decision to end things with Gene, they had disappeared when she'd finally made it to New York. He'd been furious she was late and had made him wait. She'd explained that he had been the one to book her flight, but he couldn't and wouldn't accept the blame.

He'd sat there, wearing that terribly condescending look, lecturing her about her responsibilities and her lack of attentiveness to detail.

She should have insisted they get her to New York on time. She should have called him sooner. Of course, he totally overlooked the fact she had called, but he'd been at his conference. She should have . . . .

She should never have let herself get engaged to Gene. When he talked of rescheduling their wedding, she'd told him things wouldn't work out. She didn't know why it had taken her so long to see that.

She wanted romance.

He wanted cheap.

She needed true love.

He needed to save money.

There was no way to reconcile those different wants and needs.

If he hadn't been looking for the best deal, she

would have had a direct flight to New York. If he hadn't been looking to save money, he wouldn't have planned a wedding around a conference.

Cassie deserved better than that.

She was a successful career woman who'd always managed just fine on her own. Okay, maybe there was that little problem with the IRS, but she'd taken care of it by hiring Gene.

What a dismal failure that had been.

Not that he hadn't fixed her tax problems—he had. But Gene didn't have an understanding or sympathetic bone in his body. When she told him there wouldn't be another wedding, he'd given her one of those condescending looks of his, as if he knew something she didn't.

"Well, I know I won't be marrying Gene," she told Dudley, not that he seemed interested.

Back and forth, back and forth.

"Come on, boy. You just tell Cassie what's wrong."

The dog stopped pacing right in front of the kitchen window and whined. His head was high enough to peer out through the low window, and he stared with his chocolate brown eyes at Cooper's house. Cassie swore she could see longing in Dudley's gaze.

"You liked Cooper, didn't you, Dudley? I like him too. Maybe we could invite him over for dinner? What do you think?"

Dudley's tail wagged furiously.

Cassie reached for the phone. She had a feeling that Dudley wasn't going to be happy until he saw Cooper again. And who was she to stand in the way of her dog's happiness?

She dialed the phone feeling better than she had since she'd stepped on the plane Friday morning.

Cooper pushed his plate toward the middle of the table. "Has anyone ever mentioned you're a heck of a cook?"

"I don't think that qualifies as cooking. I mean it came from a jar and a box."

Cassie debated whether or not she could possibly fit one more bite into her rather full stomach. Spaghetti was a simple but filling meal and one of her favorites.

Maybe that was why she couldn't find a man—she was a spaghetti kind of woman.

Men wanted their women more daring, more mysterious—women who liked châteaubriand or escargot.

She decided she could definitely squeeze a couple more bites in. Since she was going spend her life a single career woman, it didn't matter if she put on a few pounds. There would be no one to notice but Dudley. Since he wasn't done growing and would eventually outweigh her even if she did gain weight, she doubted he'd care.

"I think Dud's waiting for his share," Cooper said.

"I don't think spaghetti's good for a dog." She paused a moment, then added, "And don't call him Dud. You'll hurt his feelings. You're his hero. He looks up to you."

"Dogs don't have heroes."

She took one more small helping of spaghetti from the bowl. "Oh, yes they do, and you're Dudley's. It's a responsibility you can't shirk. Now, tell him you're sorry for calling him a nasty nickname."

"I'm not apologizing to a dog."

She deftly twirled her forkful of noodles. "I can't believe how unreasonable you are."

"You're just overwrought from this entire wedding thing. Maybe you and Gene can make up."

"I thought you said we weren't right for each other." She decided if she ate another bite she might explode, so she put the plate down on the linoleum.

Sure enough, Dudley liked spaghetti.

"You're not right for each other, but if losing him is making you so miserable, maybe you should give it another shot."

"I'm not miserable. I'm—" she stopped short.

She had no idea what she was. An amateur matchmaker who couldn't seem to make a match for herself, destined for a life of singleness?

"Listen, let's forget my ex-fiancé and think about ice cream."

"Ice cream?" Cooper looked skeptical.

Maybe he had never been introduced to the restorative qualities of ice cream. That was sad. It was a good thing for him that he'd moved in next door to her.

"Oh, yeah, ice cream. The store is only about a half mile, and Dudley could use the exercise."

"And you could use the ice cream?"

"Now you're catching on." She might be full, but she was never too full for ice cream. It sort of oozed into the cracks and crevices.

Feeling more confident about ice cream's abilities to improve her mood, Cassie went to find Dudley's leash. She knew she'd bought one, and that he'd had it on when he'd come into the house. Where on earth had she put it?

"Lose something, Cassie?" Cooper asked in that annoying I'm-so-organized tone he used so often.

It was a tone that reminded her why she would never even consider asking him out on a date. They were far too different to ever be more than friendly neighbors.

When he'd first moved in she'd been appreciative—he certainly improved the scenic qualities of the neighborhood. But it soon became obvious that he was of those annoyingly efficient, organized souls. And after she found out his legal specialty was divorce, well there couldn't be a more opposite profession to her own. No, there could never be more than a neighborly friendship between them.

Cassie felt even more depressed. It was going to take an awfully big ice cream cone to lift her spirits tonight.

Cooper had never thought of ice cream as a particularly sensual dessert. He'd even hoped it might cool the sudden heat that seemed to permeate his body whenever he was around Cassie.

Watching her kneeling while she searched for Dudley's leash did strange things to Cooper's thoughts.

Cassie kneeling, bending over, stretching . . . they all made him think thoughts that should never be thought about a neighbor.

A friend.

A buddy.

A pal.

No, lustful thoughts had no business being used on Cassiopeia Grant. They were too different to be anything more than friends. And he hadn't had a problem with that until today. While she had been attached to another man, there was no question of romance, but suddenly it was all too easy to remember that now she was available.

He turned to her, only to have more of those lustful thoughts as she licked her vanilla ice cream cone.

She started by the base and let her tongue roll up slowly all the way up to the top.

She smiled at him. "So what do you think?"

Cooper desperately tried to remember what they'd been talking about.

"Earth calling Cooper. I asked, what do you think?"

"About what?" he managed.

"About helping me with Dudley. You saw how he was. He won't budge on his leash for me—"

Cooper interrupted, "Once you found it."

She stuck out her tongue. "And, he's a growing puppy who needs regular exercise, so I asked if you'd consider walking him. Like I said, you're his hero."

Cooper pretended not to hear her blatant hint that he become the neighborhood dog-walker and focused instead on growing dogs. "He's still growing?"

"He's an Old English mastiff. Levi said he'd get bigger."

Cooper eyed the huge dog. Sure enough, his huge feet were disproportionate to his size. "But he must already be about one-thirty."

"One thirty-six, but who's counting? Levi said he'll be about two hundred pounds or more when he's done growing." She lovingly patted the dog's head.

"Two hundred pounds? What were you thinking? Dud's going to be a horse."

"Shh. I told you, you're going to hurt his feelings calling him that. And since I reconciled myself to a life of singleness, I don't see how two hundred pounds of dog matters much. I mean, the house is sort of big for just one person."

"Tell me about it."

Their houses were mirror images of each other, both built by the same builder. Both built for families, not for a single people.

Cooper had been thinking about buying a condo, or something more stylish, but when he'd seen this house it had felt right. The house in East Erie gave him a sense of continuity, a sense of coming home. It was part of a neighborhood with giant old trees and real neighbors.

"I like it here. It's close to the heart of Erie, and yet has a feeling of a small community. The house might be big for one person, but it feels right. The moment I walked through the door, it felt like home."

Home.

That first day, just months ago, he'd felt as if he'd been a part of the neighborhood forever. After the moving truck had pulled away, Cassie was right there, a coffee cake in hand, welcoming him to the neighborhood.

Yes, he'd felt as if he'd come home at that very moment.

"Dudley here is going to be a great watchdog," Cassie said, as if his watch-doggedness could justify keeping a beast who would grow up to be the size of a farm animal in her home.

"The only thing I see him watching is food. He eyeballed us through the entire meal, and then scarfed down his portion like a starving man."

Cooper had watched Dudley as carefully as the dog had watched the food. He was nervous that Dud would feel the need to reinitiate him. Dog's marked territory, maybe that's what Dud had been doing when he'd peed on Cooper's leg, marking him.

Well, Cooper didn't need to be marked again. As it was, he'd thrown his jeans and shoes out. He didn't want to lose any more clothing or shoes.

"Dudley's a growing boy," Cassie defended.

As if he knew they were talking about him, Dudley stopped walking and turned around to eye their ice cream cones.

Cassie shook a finger at him. "You may be growing and I might share my spaghetti with you, but you're not getting my ice cream."

"Here, you can have some of mine," Cooper said, dropping the remainder of his cone on the sidewalk. The dog made short work of it. "I think he likes ice cream more than spaghetti."

"See, I told you he was smart," Cassie said and took another huge lick of her cone.

Cooper concentrated on watching the dog. It was safer than watching Cassie.

"So, do you think you could help me out by walking Dudley sometimes?"

"I guess."

"That's great. Thanks." Cassie took off down the street again, licking her cone. Cooper fell behind a little, just to avoid the view and the thoughts it caused, but if he was behind Cassie there still was a view and it caused just as many thoughts as the ice cream cone.

"Come on, Dud," he said gruffly.

Maybe he could walk ahead of Cassie, then she'd be the one coping with the views. Only problem was, he doubted Cassie had ever had an impure thought in her life.

How a woman could grow up in the twentieth century and reach the beginning of the twenty-first, and still have an eighteenth-century innocence cloaking her like a chastity belt was beyond him. He needed to get home and clear his mind of all these weird Cassie thoughts, so he picked up the pace.

"Something wrong, Cooper?" Cassie called, as he hurried down the street.

"I'm just in a hurry to get home. I've got some calls to make. It seems I'm never done with work."

"What you need is a date," Cassie said.

"Isn't that rather like the pot calling the kettle black? I mean, a woman who's bound and determined to be a spinster shouldn't be so determined to marry off someone else."

"I've decided not to call myself a spinster. I'm using career woman, as in a woman whose focus is advancing her career. So, maybe I've decided to marry myself to my job, but that doesn't mean I won't date. It only means that I'd given up on finding an ever-after-love."

Something in Cooper winced at her sad tone. He'd mocked her romantic streak in the past, but he hated the idea of Cassie losing it. Even if he didn't believe in love like that, maybe he needed for Cassie to believe.

Suddenly he had an idea. An idea about how to get Cassie out of her funk, and move her safely into the belongs-to-someone-else, unavailable category again.

"Hey, remember my buddy, Leo? He helped me move in?"

She nodded.

"Seems he was disappointed when you told him you were engaged. Maybe I could set you two up and play matchmaker for a change."

The moment he said the words he regretted them. Leo was a body builder. He spent so much time building his body that he was bound to notice Cassie's body. And if Leo noticed Cassie's body, he was bound to have the same sort of fantasies that had been plaguing Cooper. And if he had those kind of fantasies, he might try to act on them.

"Wait," he said, ready to rescind the suggestion.

But Cassie was already nodding her head yes.

"Okay, but only if I can set you up with someone as well. We'll all go out together."

"Double date?" he mused.

That could work. He could be sure that it would be a horrible date for Cassie and Leo. That Leo's body-loving thoughts stayed off Cassie's body. "Sure. That's a great idea."

She looked surprised at his quick response. "When? Next week?"

Cooper nodded. "Next week. You and me on a double date."

Maybe seeing her with another man would be enough to make him forget these weird thoughts about her he'd been having.

He hoped so.

Cassie was smiling as she went into WLVH that evening. She felt more like herself than she had since the whole elopement had gone bad.

She definitely remembered Leo. A professional bodybuilder who wrote poetry in his spare time. A true renaissance man.

She knew just the woman for him. She'd been waiting to see him at Cooper's again to set things up. This double date would work even better.

She'd call Fran tomorrow.

She was whistling when she walked into the snack room and tossed a cup of water in the microwave.

She was surprised to when Craig walked into the room.

"You're here late," she said, taking the now-hot water out of the microwave and dropping a teabag into the cup.

"Levi said you adopted the dog."

She nodded. "He's just what the doctor ordered."

"Speaking of the doctor, I know you said you were done with love—"

"I am." She might be feeling more optimistic, more like herself, but that hadn't changed.

"But you're not done with dating, are you?"

His question echoed what she'd just said to Cooper.

"No," she answered slowly.

"Great. Because Ted and I came up with a fantastic new promotion for our Splash Bash. I mean, after Punch and Judy's wedding last year, we need something big for this year's."

Cassie didn't say anything, she just stared at Craig. He wasn't just smiling. He looked almost . . . jovial. And jovial wasn't a word she'd ever used to describe Craig before.

"Don't you want to hear my idea?"

"I don't think so," she said. "I remember Ted's ideas for Punch and Judy. They weren't happy, and I doubt I'll like his ideas any more than they did."

"We're going to find you a date for the bash. We'll start running the ads next week. Men have to send us a letter telling the station why you should go out with them."

"No."

"You know the old saying about falling off the horse and getting back on again," Craig said.

"No."

"Oh, come on. You can pick the horse you get onto!"

"I'm not getting on anyone," Cassie assured him.

He looked embarrassed. "That's not what I meant. I mean, you're single again. This is an easy way to get back in the dating circuit."

"I don't know if I have time. I mean, things are busy at the station, and I do have Dudley now. He's going to require a lot of time."

"Cassie." Frustration tinged his voice.

"No."

Craig wasn't jovial. Wasn't embarrassed or even frustrated. No, suddenly he was very military. "This isn't a question, it's an order. The station needs a contest, and win-a-date-with-Cassie is that contest."

"You're sure you want to order me?" Cassie asked.

"Yes."

"Fine. Just remember you asked for it."

Craig had the sense to look nervous, but he quickly covered it with his sergeant demeanor. "Good."

Cassie would do his stupid contest and pick a date . . . but she wasn't going to be the only one.

She might be a dog-owning, permanently single career woman, but she was ready to prove she still believed in love for other people. First she had the double date with Coop, and now she had this opportunity at the station.

Cassiopeia Grant was back in the game and ready for some serious matchmaking.

Craig might be annoyed at first, but she hoped he thanked her someday.

Chapter Three

"*You* all know WLVH is planning its Second Annual Splash Bash—A way to see the summer out in a big way. This year, Night Calls and WLVH are having a contest. Some of you have heard me talk about Craig, my new station manager. He's as confirmed a bachelor as I am a newly confirmed bachelorette. But we both enjoy dating. So, all you eligible bachelors and bachelorettes, send us a page-long essay on why you would be our perfect dates. Craig and I will each pick one lucky entrant for a night on the town after our Second Annual Splash Bash, courtesy of WLVH and Night Calls, where we live by the motto: love is more than just a song."

"Come on, Cassie," Cooper called again.

When she'd suggested they drive to dinner together, Cooper should have known better than to agree.

Cassie was running late.

No surprise there. Cassie would probably find a way to be late for her own funeral and Cooper knew it wouldn't surprise anyone. It was a funeral that could arrive sooner than she'd anticipated if she didn't hurry up.

"Come on," he called again.

"I'm coming. I just need to find my left white pump," she called from her bedroom.

Cooper might have offered to help if she was searching for something in any room other than her bedroom. But the thoughts of entering Cassie's bedroom made him decidedly uncomfortable.

He wasn't sure why he was suddenly plagued with all these odd feelings concerning Cassie, but he wasn't about to analyze it.

He was a man and he could be as irrational as any woman if he felt like it. And when it came to entering Cassie's bedroom, he felt like it. The mere thought made him uncomfortable. Almost as uncomfortable as the mastiff who was sitting on his foot.

"Come on, Dud, move your big butt."

"What a way to talk to an impressionable baby who worships you," Cassie said as she entered the room.

At that moment, any retort lay frozen in Cooper's throat as his brain ceased working.

He might have only known Cassiopeia Grant for two months, might have eaten countless meals in her home, might have even shared the occasional evening of television or videos with her, but he hardly recognized the woman standing before him.

His Cassie—well, not *his* Cassie, but the Cassie he'd grown to know and even like when she wasn't setting him up—was a down-to-earth sort of woman. A blond pixie with a quick smile and a generous heart. A woman more at home in T-shirts and jeans than fancy clothes. He'd never seen her in anything dressier than the occasional pair of khakis.

No, this creature was anything but down to earth. If he were a poetic sort of man—which, thank goodness he wasn't—he might be tempted to say that Cassiopeia Grant was quite heavenly.

The white dress she wore was made of some gauzy sort of material. A good gust of wind and the thing would practically blow away. But the more he looked, the more he started to hate the dress.

Why, it was way to short. Okay, so maybe it almost reached her knees, and that wouldn't bother him on any other woman, but on Cassie it didn't look good. And the vee of the neckline was far too low.

It wasn't just T-shirts she was prone to wear, but baggy T-shirts that hid everything.

"I'll take the fact you've stared at me for," she glanced at her watch, "a full minute and twenty seconds as a compliment."

"Compliment?"

Maybe it would have been a compliment for any other woman, but not Cassie.

No way was she going to dinner with that macho-man Leo in that getup. What on earth was he thinking when he set this whole thing up?

Cooper might not know what he'd been thinking, but he knew exactly what Leo would be thinking when he saw Cassie in that dress. No way was he going to have Leo thinking those thoughts all through dinner.

"What are you thinking wearing that dress in public?" he asked.

"I'm not in public yet," she reminded him. Then, plucking nervously at a sleeve, added, "And what's wrong with my dress?"

"There's not nearly enough of it, for one thing."

"You've got to be kidding. It practically reaches my knees."

"Well, there's that, but I was referring to the fact that I can see your . . ." he paused, having trouble getting the word out, "well, the V-neck is just too low. Leo might get the wrong idea about you."

"What on earth has gotten into you, Cooper? This date with Leo was your idea."

"Well, maybe it was a bad idea, as bad an idea as your wearing the dress in public."

"You're not my mother. Who do you think you are, telling me what I can and cannot wear?"

"I'm the man who's driving you on this date, and I'm not going to be embarrassed by you exposing your . . ." he stumbled over the word again.

"Cleavage," she said. "Come on, *cleavage.* You must have seen countless women's cleavage by now, so I'm sure you can say the word."

"I don't want to say the word, and I certainly don't want to look at yours all night."

Cassie had told him about the friend she'd fixed him up with, Fran the librarian.

Cooper would bet Fran wasn't flaunting cleavage. Why the poor woman would probably be scandalized to see Cassie parading around like this, flaunting things she had no right even owning.

"At least my shushing librarian—"

"She has a name. It's Fran."

"—is apt to be fully covered."

"My dress is perfectly decent. And since when did you become keeper of my conscience and closet?"

"Since we adopted a dog together."

"We didn't adopt Dudley. *I* adopted Dudley. He just likes you."

"Well, since I've volunteered to help walk him, I have a vested interest in Dud, and I'm not about to have his mother parading all over downtown Erie half dressed."

"I'm fully dressed and you can—"

"Please?" The word stopped her arguments cold. Muttering about stupid men, Cassie stormed back into her bedroom.

Cooper grinned. He might be as half-witted as Cassie said, but he'd just won the argument. He reached down and pet the dog, who was still firmly planted on his now rather numb foot. "We can't have your Mom walking around town like some kind of call girl, can we?"

The dog panted and a huge slimy drool dropped onto the foot Dud wasn't sitting on. Cooper might have been annoyed if Dudley hadn't helped him win the battle, but since the dog had been the deciding factor, he decided to overlook his slimy shoe.

Shoes.

Cassie had managed to find her white pumps, but they didn't go with any other outfit than this one. Now she'd have to search for another pair just because Cooper had some bee in his bonnet about her outfit.

There was nothing wrong with this dress. It was perfectly respectable. Not that Cooper thought so. But then, who'd asked him?

Not her, that's for sure.

Cassie started searching through her closet for another suitable dress.

They were going to be late.

She pulled out the blue cocktail dress she'd worn to Marilyn and Mark's wedding. It was far too dressy for tonight. She seemed to have two choices in her closet: Ultra-wedding-dressy or jeans. There was no middle ground.

Darn. She was going shopping next week. It would serve Cooper, the unreasonable fashion critic, right if she dragged him along.

She pulled out a black slip dress. It had a higher scoop neckline—a neckline that wouldn't show the slightest hint of cleavage. And it was longer. The thing came all the way to her knees.

All it left exposed was her arms, and Cooper certainly couldn't object to her arms. He couldn't object. This dress would do just fine.

"Cassie, come on. Dud's drooling all over me as well as shedding all over my suit. Your librarian's shushing is likely to kick up a cloud of dog hair," his royal majesty bellowed from her living room.

"I'm coming," she called. "This change of clothes was your idea, not mine, so just shut up and let me get on with it."

She slid the dress over her head. "And now I have to find my black pumps and that could take hours."

There. She'd told him.

Cooper decided it was a good thing they were double dating. Cassie obviously needed a keeper. But did she have to fix him up with a librarian?

He imagined his date. She was probably a lot safer than his neighbor. She was probably prematurely gray and wearing spectacles—not glasses, spectacles. And most important, she was probably wearing one of those iron reinforced bras under a hideous gray dress that started at her neck and practically reached her ankles.

The image was almost soothing after the new look Cassie showed him.

"I'm ready."

He turned, expecting to find his old Cassie waiting for him.

"No, you're not," he said when he saw her.

She was wearing black now. A black slip thing that belonged under a dress, not as a dress.

"No way. You're even more naked than last time."

"Are you nuts? It reaches my knees."

"It's still . . ." Cooper paused, unsure what his complaint was with this dress. But she still didn't look right. She still didn't look like herself.

"You could wear your khaki pants," he offered in a very helpful manner.

He should have thought of it before. Pants were perfect. Cassie would look like herself in pants.

"Bite me, Cooper. I'm wearing this dress. The only thing showing is my arms, and I don't think they're that big a turn on."

They weren't a turn off either, and that was the problem, Cooper realized. He'd never noticed, until this moment, that her elbows were part of two of the sexiest arms he'd ever seen.

"Maybe you'd better take a sweater?" he suggested.

"If I take a sweater will you stop this nonsense so we can get this show on the road?"

"Sure."

He wasn't even going to argue the word *nonsense*. He was only thinking of Cassie's virtue.

"Fine. I'm taking a sweater, but I'm not wearing it. It's too hot."

Cooper decided he was feeling hot as well. Hot enough to need the air-conditioning in his car turned on at full blast.

"We're late," Cooper grumbled as they walked into the restaurant a short drive later.

"And whose fault would that be?" She said smugly, knowing for once it wasn't hers. She'd almost forgotten she'd intended to be late, and that Cooper had merely helped.

"It was your fault," he muttered as the hostess came over. "The Cooper party," he said.

"Simms. The reservation was under Simms."

Cooper glared at her, but said nothing.

Unaware of the tension, the hostess merely nodded. "The rest of your party is here." Picking up two menus, she led them into the back room.

"My fault?" Cassie hissed, unwilling to let the topic die.

"If you'd had the sense to dress like . . ."

"Like what?" she practically growled. "Like a

nun? Because that's how I feel. Don't think you fooled me. I know you turned the air-conditioning on high to force me to wear this darned sweater, but it won't work. The restaurant isn't sub-Arctic."

"What if I simply apologize? Cassie, I'm sorry. Maybe I'm nervous about these dates and it caused me to be a bit overbearing."

"A bit?"

"A lot."

"Dork," she whispered, but there wasn't a lot of ire left in the word. Cooper was just being Cooper. She'd decided right after she met him that he'd become an attorney in order to get paid to fight. He liked to debate issues. When he started in on her dress she should have realized he was nervous about tonight and she could have started to talk about politics with him.

Fighting about politics always seemed to soothe him.

"Don't be nervous." She reached over and squeezed his hand. "We're going to have a nice time tonight."

They reached the table. "Hi, Leo," she said brightly. "I see you found Fran."

"Actually Fran found me."

Cassie purposely took the seat next to Fran, leaving Cooper the seat next to Leo. She pretended not to notice Cooper's frown. "I hope you didn't mind waiting. You see, when Cooper's not at the courthouse, he's busy critiquing my outfits. He wanted me to look my best tonight."

"Oh, you're a lawyer?" Fran asked.

Was that disappointment in Fran's voice? Cassie sure hoped so. She'd met Leo when Cooper had moved in and she realized there was more to him than bodybuilding. A lot more.

She knew Fran in a casual sort of way. But she had a feeling she might be just the type of woman Leo was looking for, which is why she'd set Fran up with Cooper.

She didn't tell Cooper that little fact. He'd just get testy. He wouldn't like to think of himself as a matchmaker, but the thought made her smile.

"Oh, Cooper's an attorney all right," she said. "Briefs, cases—why, work is about all he talks about."

"Can I get you something from the bar?" the waitress asked.

"The bar. Cooper knows about the bar," Cassie bubbled. Leo and Fran looked confused. "In a lawyer sort of way, of course. Why, Cooper isn't an alcoholic, or anything . . ."

"At least not yet," he muttered, shooting her a look that said he questioned her sanity.

"A Coke," he said with more volume for the waitress's benefit.

"Ice water with lemon," Cassie added.

"We're fine," Leo and Fran said in unison. They laughed together as well.

"We were talking about art before you two got here," Leo said.

"You both like art?" Cassie asked.

"Oh, we love it. There's a great collection at the museum and Fran and I were thinking about going this weekend—" Leo cut himself off suddenly, realizing he was supposed to be out with Cassie. He blushed and started to stutter, "Oh, Cassie, I'm sorry. That was so rude. I mean, I'm supposed to be here with you and—"

"Leo, this was Cooper's idea. What does Cooper know? He's just a divorce lawyer with a bad case of fashion-criticitis. What does he know about what sort of people click? This was more a casual get-together than a date so you're not going to hurt my feelings if you go to an exhibit with Fran."

The waitress brought their drinks.

"Thank you," Cassie said.

When she was gone, Cassie continued, "And Fran, I haven't been able to find anyone who would suit Cooper. He's not an easy man, you know. But I've so enjoyed talking to you at the library, I thought if nothing else this might be a way to get to know you better. But I have to confess, it doesn't surprise me a bit that you two hit it off. As a matter of fact, I have a feeling about you and Leo, don't you Coop?"

Cooper didn't say a word.

"Feelings aren't very reliable," Fran pointed out.

"Actually, if you think about it, feelings are all we have. What makes someone fall in love? There's no scientific or quantitative way to measure it, or even attempt to predict it. So, when I say I have a feeling about the two of you, it's as accurate as any other means of predicting when two people will click."

"So you don't mind that Fran and I are going out?" Leo asked.

"Not a bit. We'll just swap partners. Cooper here, since he picked my dress, can be my date and enjoy his handiwork, and you and Fran can get to know each other."

"Guess things didn't work out the way you planned, Cooper." Leo chuckled deeply.

Cooper had been listening to that annoying rumble from the literary giant all night. He'd grown to really hate the sound. A bodybuilding, poetry spouting, art fanatic was more than any man should have to deal with. But no, Cooper had dealt with Leo for the entire two hours—he checked his watch—and forty-three minute meal.

Fran, the I-am-a-knockout librarian, hadn't even had the decency to shush anyone throughout the entire meal. As a matter of fact, she'd gotten almost loud during her discussion of pointillism with Leo. Cooper had been tempted to shush her himself.

But even Fran the librarian wasn't Cooper's

biggest hurdle. No, it was Miss "sexy arms" Grant. Cooper swore she was flaunting her elbows just to torment him.

Things hadn't turn out the way he'd anticipated?

"No, I guess you could say they didn't," he told Leo. "But, I'm glad you and Fran hit it off."

"Thanks for being such a sport." Fran stood on tip-toes and kissed his cheek. "Maybe the four of us could double again?"

Yeah, when hell froze over; when Dudley stopped sliming; when Cassie stopped driving him crazy. Maybe then, but not a second before.

"That would be lovely," Cassie said. "But I doubt Cooper and I are destined for many dates."

"Really?" Fran asked. "That's funny because I had a feeling that there was something between you."

"A hundred and thirty-six-pound puppy would be about it," Cassie assured her.

"Funny, I thought the two of you looked good together too," Leo added. He shrugged. "I guess you were right Cassie. There's no way to tell which two people will click, and which ones won't." So saying, he wrapped his arm around Fran, and walked her across the parking lot.

"I have to thank you, Cooper," Cassie said as she and Cooper watched Fran and Leo walk off.

Instead of reaping her gratitude, Cooper asked, "You don't have a feeling in the world about us?"

"You can relax, there's not even the slightest

nudge. And like I said, I have to thank you. Fran was right, you were a real good sport tonight."

"Not the slightest nudge?"

"No, so you can relax." She opened the passenger door and crawled into his car. Right before the door closed, Cooper got another healthy look at her arm . . . darn, she had great elbows.

Relax? He stormed around to his own side of the car and climbed in. How was he supposed to relax with his single and sexy neighbor sitting next to him for the fifteen minute ride home? He had to contend with her arms flapping around the car, all bare and sexy.

He turned on the cold air, full blast.

But even as Cassie slipped on her sweater, Cooper knew a mere scrap of knit cotton wasn't going to solve his problem. No. The only thing that was going to fix things between them was if she got involved in a new relationship.

"Are you going to say something?" Cassie asked after five minutes of silence.

"What do you want me to say?"

"You could start with something like, 'You were right, Cassie.' "

"Right about what?"

"Well, we could start with Fran. She didn't shush you once the entire meal."

"After the first five minutes she wasn't my date anymore, she was Leo the bodybuilding poet's date. She's probably shushing him right now."

"The only way she'd be shushing him would be to get him to quiet down for a proper good-night kiss. Speaking of them kissing—"

Cooper would rather they didn't speak of kissing, but Cassie just barreled along, unconcerned.

"—when I get my wedding invitation, would you like to go with me? After all, you played a role in getting the two of them together."

"I thought you said we wouldn't be dating again."

Not even a twinge of a feeling about him, she'd said that too.

"We never really dated in the first place, so it would be hard to date again."

"Why haven't we ever dated? We've shared a ton of meals. We're even sharing our slimy dog."

"*My* slimy dog. He just likes you. And we've shared meals because we're neighbors."

"Neighbors? You think that's all we are?"

"Of course we're more than neighbors. We're friends." She reached across the car and laid her hand on his arm. "Why else would I be trying to find you someone?"

Cooper wished his Mustang had more width to it, anything that would keep more distance between him and Cassie. "Why else would you try to find me someone? Because you're a meddlesome kind of lady who has rose-colored glasses and a fairy tale perception of love?"

"What's wrong with my perception of love?"

"It's not real life. Real life relationships aren't based on your *feelings*. They're based on a sense of mutual attraction, with a sprinkling of common interests."

"I've built my radio show on feelings. That's why people call me, they trust in my feelings. But not you, right? Attraction and interests matter in a relationship, but not feelings?"

Cooper didn't need to be able to see Cassie to know she was disappointed in him. He could hear it in her sigh.

"No wonder none of your dates pan out. No woman wants a man who denies he has feelings."

"So you're saying women prefer poetry-spouting jocks like Leo Simms?"

"No. I'm saying a woman wants a man who's honest with her, and maybe more importantly, honest with himself. If you deny having feelings, then you're neither."

Cooper shut up. There was no way he was going to win this argument, so why bother? Cassie was wrong. She didn't want him to be honest about his feelings.

If he was honest he'd turn to her and say, *Your arms are driving me nuts. I want to pull over in some secluded spot and make out like teenagers.*

And if he was going to be truly honest he'd say, *And your romantic view of love scares me, which is why the last thing I'd ever do is follow through on that impulse.*

Cooper was awash with relief when his car finally pulled into his driveway. Some piece of misplaced chivalry forced him to wait for Cassie to get out of the car and walk with her to her door.

"You don't have to do this," she said, breaking the silence.

"Do what?"

"Walk me to my door. I'm perfectly capable of walking across the lawn on my own."

"Just get your keys and get in the house so I can go home. I have to be at court at eight tomorrow."

"Why are you so mad at me?" She fumbled in her purse, looking for her keys.

"A better question might be why can't you keep track of anything? We were late to dinner because you couldn't get ready on time—"

"That's not fair, you're the one who made me change."

"—and you're forever losing keys, losing perfectly good fiancés, and . . ." Cooper searched his mind for other negative Cassie-qualities, needing to make a list of all the reasons he should run in the opposite direction from the attraction he was suddenly feeling for his flighty, fluff-ball of a neighbor.

"And I'm sure you bought yourself such a big dog because you were afraid you'd lose a poodle, just like you lose or misplace everything else."

Cassie had stopped rooting through her purse and just stared at him.

Well, let her stare away, Cooper wasn't done yet. "You know, I think the whole blond theory has merit."

"I don't know why you're being so mean, you, you . . . you dork."

"You wanted feelings, well, now you know what mine are. You make me crazy."

"What on earth have I ever done to you?" Her voice was close to a whisper, and she still stood, hands motionless in her purse, staring at him.

"You want to know?" he shouted. "You really want to know?"

"Yes!"

"Since I moved in, I've thought of you as a neighbor. A cute little, *engaged* friend. We've shared laughs and the occasional meal. But tonight you changed all that, and I'll confess, I'm not happy about it."

All these *feelings* and these lurid little pictures in his imagination that had plagued him all evening were Cassie's fault.

"How? I've set you up on half a dozen dates before, what's so different tonight? Are you mad because I never really thought you and Fran would suit each other? I'm sorry if you feel manipulated, I didn't mean to hurt you, I just—"

"Cassie, I never gave Fran a second look, though she was the antithesis of a stereotypical-looking librarian. Maybe, if it wasn't for you, I would have looked twice."

He thought back to his nonmousy librarian, the woman who had almost been his date and added, "Maybe even three times. That I didn't is your fault too."

"You still haven't told me what I did to make you so mad."

"You came out of your room tonight and suddenly you weren't my *engaged* neighbor, you were a gorgeous, unattached woman. And I hate that. I can't decide if I hate the gorgeous, or the unattached part more."

"I—"

He held up his hand, unwilling to be reasonable. He was definitely feeling unreasonable. "Don't try to deny it. You have cleavage."

"I changed," she protested.

"Yeah, you changed all right. Changed from my buddy to a woman."

"I mean, I changed clothes."

"Oh, just find your keys so I can go home. Blond."

"Well, you're not blond, but there's definitely something wrong with your mental process," she muttered as she dug through her purse.

What on earth had come over Cooper? She'd thought he was her friend, but he was obviously now just the lunatic who lived next door.

Poor Dudley. He was going to be brokenhearted that they didn't see Cooper anymore. Maybe she could take the dog to visit at whatever insane asylum Cooper ended up living in.

"Come on, Cassie," he growled.

"I'm looking!" she shouted. The shout ended in a pathetic little hitch.

Rats, she was crying. There was nothing Cassie hated more than crying. Her Grandma Rose use to say when you found something you were good at, you should do it with abandon, but Cassie wasn't about to cry with abandon in front of her lunatic neighbor, no matter how good she was at it.

"You're not crying, are you?" Cooper asked.

"No," she blatantly lied, and frantically continued digging for her keys. She could hear Dudley scratching and whining on the other side of the door.

"You are crying," he whispered. Gently, he touched her cheek. "Cassie, I'm sorry."

She jerked her head away from his touch. "Don't do that."

"Do what?"

"Don't go back to pretending you're a nice guy, that you're my friend. What you are is, is . . ."

"I'm sorry. Really."

"Yeah. I'm just your blond neighbor who loses everything from keys to fiancés."

That hurt. She hadn't actually lost Gene. She'd simply broken things off with him after their wedding debacle.

"I hurt you, didn't I?" Cooper asked softly, as if all his anger had finally bled away.

"Yes, you hurt me. And I really don't understand why."

"It made me mad."

"What?" She hadn't done a single thing to him— at least not that she could think of. She'd been wracking her brain the entire ride home, but she couldn't think of a single thing.

"Tonight, you went from being a safely engaged neighbor, to . . ."

"To what?" she pressed.

"To a woman I want to do this to . . ."

Chapter Four

"Cassie, this is Joshua. I'm faxing over a letter now, hoping you'll choose me to be your Splash Bash date. Like I say in the letter, I'm in my mid-thirties and ready to settle down with the right woman. I'd be loyal and good company. A real gentleman who's ready to take things slow and easy . . ."

Cassie didn't move as Cooper wrapped her in his arms, then slow and easy, he pulled her closer. She read his intent. Rather than pull away, she leaned into him and became a willing participant in the kiss.

Kiss?

That was the understatement of the century. The touch of his lips to hers was magic. It was poetry. It was every fantasy Cassie had ever had, and then some. It was everything a kiss should be.

Her only thought was to get closer, to prolong the moment of ecstasy for eternity, to get her hands out of her purse so she could wrap them around Cooper's neck and never let go.

But before she'd managed to disentangle herself from her purse, Cooper was ending the kiss and backing up, rubbing his lips as if hers had been covered with chili peppers and the effect was burning him.

"I've got to go," he choked out.

Finally, her hands were free, but Cooper had slipped from her grasp. "Maybe we should talk."

"I think there's been enough talking tonight. Enough of everything." He turned and bolted over the bush that divided their driveways.

Cooper might have thought they'd experienced enough of everything tonight, but as Cassie let herself into the house she was pretty sure they hadn't experienced nearly enough.

An hour later there was a knock on the door.

Cooper?

He'd come back. That was Cassie's first thought as she rushed to open the door.

After their stupefying kiss, she'd come into the house, let Dudley slobber his happiness to see her all over her. Then she'd taken a cold shower—a very cold shower—to wash off the dog kisses and try to erase the sense of longing that had set in the minute Cooper's lips left hers.

The shower didn't help.

Cassie had a feeling that nothing would help ease the tightness in her chest except another dose from the *cause* of these feelings.

There was another knock.

The *cause* had returned.

Excited, she paused and glanced in the mirror in the entryway.

Darn. She should have foregone the cold shower, especially if Cooper was back to pick up where they'd left off. But, there was no help for it. Cooper had seen her without makeup before, and the nice thing about having short hair was a few rakes of her fingers through it and it was essentially styled.

"Hi," she said as she opened the door. Instead of beating to the cadence of her excitement, her heart sank.

"Hello, Cassie."

Average brown hair that was perfectly styled even this late at night, glasses perched just so and casually dressed—which for him meant khaki trousers and a polo shirt—Gene Gifford stood on her front porch grinning.

What a night. First a kissing, insane runaway neighbor, then a nearly forgotten ex-fiancé shows up at her door.

Could things get any worse?

Probably.

A terrible feeling of foreboding swept through her. Oh, yeah, things could get plenty worse.

Forcing a sense of congeniality into her voice, Cassie tried to match Gene's smile. "What a surprise. What are you doing here?"

Gene strode into the house as if he owned it.

Unfortunately, Dudley wasn't prepared for any visitors other than Cooper, and came tearing through the hall, bumping into Gene and sent him sprawling inelegantly onto the floor.

"What on earth?" Gene looked rather faint beneath the huge puppy.

Never having met an intruder he didn't like, Dudley, a dog never destined for watchdoghood, proceeded to revive Gene in the best way his puppy being knew how.

Dudley slicked slimy kisses all over Gene's face, not sparing his glasses, which were soon muck-encrusted.

"Get it off me," Gene bellowed.

Cassie had been momentarily frozen, watching the scene that unfolded with a mixture of horror and humor.

Yes, things could get worse, much worse.

"Dudley, sit," she finally managed.

Dudley, for all his slimy, leash-averse ways, obviously had learned this command from his previous owner, Levi.

He sat down . . . right on Gene's sprawled legs.

"I'm so sorry," Cassie muttered as she grabbed the puppy's collar and tried to pull him off her ex-fiancé, whose face was turning that bright shade of red that indicated he was becoming annoyed.

More than annoyed.

Gene Gifford was becoming severely pissed off.

Thinking about that particular term made Cassie renew her efforts to budge the dog, fearful Gene's skyrocketing blood pressure would make him pop a heart valve if the puppy decided to initiate him the same way he'd initiated Cooper.

"Come on, Dudley. Let's go look for doggie bones in the kitchen."

Bones must have been a magic word, because Dudley was up in a flash.

"Let me just put Dudley away," she called as Dudley raced for the kitchen. "I'll be right back. Make yourself at home."

Why on earth was Gene here?

Cassie supposed she was about to find out. She wrapped Dudley's leash to the basement door handle and clipped the other end onto his collar.

"You stay here," she commanded and tossed him a handful of dog biscuits for good measure.

Time to face Gene.

Feeling like Joan of Arc marching to her pyre, she walked into the living room and took a seat on the couch, opposite Gene.

"Gene. What brings you out this late at night?"

Dudley must have finished his biscuits because he started broadcasting a low keening sound of puppy agony.

Gene glared in the direction of the kitchen, but the look softened when he turned to Cassie.

"I missed you. I called earlier, but when I couldn't reach you, I decided to come over and talk to you in person, hoping by now you've learned your lesson."

Dudley's keening whine rose in volume and was accompanied by a scratching sound that didn't bode well for Cassie's basement door. She might have got up and tried to put a stop to the puppy nonsense, but she was more annoyed by Gene's last comment than any scratched door.

"Learned my lesson?"

Gene nodded. "You had to learn to be more responsible, so I broke off the engagement temporarily, hoping you'd learn your lesson and that when we got married, I would have a prompt and punctual wife."

"That's so unfair. The plane was late . . . a plane trip you booked. And, for the record, *I* broke off the engagement. Listen, Gene . . ."

He leaned forward as if he was going to try and oblige and really listen.

Heartened, Cassie pushed back her annoyance at his comments. She would give him the benefit of the doubt. He was just distraught because their relationship had ended. Trying to be sympathetic, she continued, "Listen, you're a great guy. It just couldn't ever work between us. We're just lucky we found out before the wedding."

He held up his hand and cut her off. "I don't think we did find out. You just had a case of cold feet. If you're honest, I think you'll find you've missed me. I know I've missed you." He reached into his pocket. "I brought you back your ring."

Cassie didn't touch the velvet box he extended to her. "Gene, I'm sorry, but . . ."

Cassie searched for how to say what she had to say. If she was brutally honest she would tell him that she hadn't missed him at all. The thought that last week she was planning to marry a man she didn't even miss when he was gone didn't say much about her character.

She'd gotten so caught up in her dream of finding someone to love that she'd allowed herself to believe that the man of her dreams was Gene Gifford. But it turned out he wasn't the man of her dreams, or even a man of her afterthoughts.

But she couldn't hurt Gene by telling him that. She might not have loved Gene the way a woman should love the man she's going to marry, but she had always liked him despite his occasional pompous attitude.

"Gene, I'm sorry things didn't work out, but I've thought about this and have come to the conclusion that the fact my flight was delayed, giving me time to really think, was a sign."

"A sign?"

Dudley's keening evolved to a louder wail.

Cassie nodded. "A sign that we were never meant to be together."

"Meant to be?" Gene asked, looking puzzled.

"As in destiny, or as in finding the other half of your whole, as in true and everlasting love."

"Cassie, we're both adults here." A loud yelp followed by an equally loud thump caused Gene to stop a moment. He scowled at Cassie, as if Dudley's bad behavior was somehow her fault, and continued. "I know you spend your nights playing the love doctor on your little show, but you have to realize that relationships have more to do with compatibility than some romantic notion of love."

"I have to?" Suddenly she wasn't feeling nearly as bad for Gene. Nope. Her sympathy had evaporated. All that was left was a feeling of annoyance.

Another thump followed by more wailing.

This time Gene just talked louder. "Of course. Marriage is, well, it's like a contract. Two people make certain binding promises. I'm willing to forgive you and you can forgive me. We'll put this behind us and start over. Like I said, I called earlier to talk to you about all this, but you weren't home. Where were you?"

Cassie was still trying to digest Gene's contract

analogy—it sounded like something Cooper would say—and his change of subject threw her.

Where was she tonight?

Without a thought, she simply blurted out, "On a date."

"I heard about that date contest on your show. That's one of the reasons I decided it was time to straighten things out sooner rather than later. But a date tonight?" Gene pulled off his glasses and as he wiped leftover Dudley smudges with tissue he'd pulled from his pocket. "With . . . ?"

Gene Gifford had never loved her, had seen their wedding as a mere formal contract. What had she been thinking? She was supposed to be an expert on love. Callers came to her with their problems and trusted her feelings to help them through their troubles. And yet she'd been willing to join her future to a man who didn't believe in love?

Had she been that desperate to marry?

She should have known Gene wasn't right for her early on. She'd mistaken undemanding friendship for love.

Thinking of Cooper's kiss, Cassie realized just how wrong she had been. She definitely was capable of having all kinds of feelings about her own relationships with men.

A particularly loud howl followed by a series of thumps pulled Cassie from her disquieting thoughts.

"Cassie?" Gene asked, practically shouting to be heard over the very annoyed puppy.

Cassie had no idea what Gene had asked. "Pardon?"

"This is another annoying habit of yours that you have to outgrow."

Cassie didn't argue that there would never be a marriage, at least between the two of them. She merely asked, "What habit?"

"Your habit of drifting off in the middle of a conversation. I asked, who were you out with? A date, like a girls night out, with one of your girlfriends?"

Cassie didn't bother to mention that this wasn't a two-way conversation, but a one-way lecture. "Actually I'm not sure how to answer that."

Yowl. Thump. Thump.

"It's a simple question, Cassie, and it deserves a simple answer."

Thump. Yowl. Thump. Yowl.

"Dudley, hush up," Cassie shouted. "But the answer isn't all that simple. I was actually out with Leo, but it was Cooper who kissed me."

She realized what she'd said and wished she could rewind and edit out the kissing part.

Actually, replaying the kissing part had been the reason she'd been forced to take a cold shower.

Dudley's howling evolved yet again, this time to a series of yips, followed by a bark much deeper than most puppies possessed.

Yip, yip. Thump. Bark.

Unfortunately there was no instant replay and edit. Gene's face was an even more vivid shade of red than when Dudley had played greeter.

"You kissed Cooper?" he asked incredulously. "You kissed the neighbor who you couldn't seem to get rid of?"

Cassie didn't consider it worth mentioning that she'd never actually tried to get rid of Cooper.

She merely said, "Yes."

"How could you kiss someone else when you belong to me?"

"Gene, I never belonged to you, even when we were engaged, and—I'm sorry but I have to point this out—whatever there was between us was severed when the engagement ended."

Yip. Thump. Yowl. Bark, bark.

"Dudley, hush," Cassie shouted. She wasn't sure who was more annoying, her misbehaving puppy, or her rather dense ex-fiancé.

"I don't believe it," Gene shouted, since Dudley hadn't hushed.

Cassie was sure she could make him believe if she described how that one kiss had affected her. How it had rocked her world, moved the earth beneath her feet. How it had awakened feelings she'd never known she possessed. But she wouldn't try to convince Gene because she didn't want to hurt him, and because the experience was too new to be shared, too sweet to be believed.

"I'm sorry, Gene. But if you're honest with yourself, you'll admit that our relationship was missing something. If I'd loved you the way you deserve to be loved, I'd never have had second thoughts." And she would have suffered without him. But she hadn't missed him at all.

Hoooowwwwl.

"Gene, the engagement's off. There isn't going to be a wedding. I'd like to think we can both be adults about this."

"Adults? You don't have the slightest clue what it is to be a responsible, mature adult."

"Maybe not," she agreed with a smile.

If being an adult meant being as stuffy as Gene, then maybe adulthood wasn't all it was cracked up to be.

She rose. "I'd like to thank you for asking me to marry you all over again. I hope you find a woman who makes you long for more than an adult relationship, more than just a marriage that's a contract. I just know that woman isn't me."

Thump. Thump. Thump.

The absence of howling made Cassie slightly nervous, as the thumping quickly picked up its tempo.

Without Dudley's vocalization, Gene's voice dropped back into the a more normal range. "So, you're going to go back to kissing your neighbor, and dating two men in one evening?"

"I don't plan on dating more than one man again. That part of the evening was a fluke."

But the kiss? She was hoping there was no fluke about that, despite the fact Cooper had run like a bat out of hell after that one monumentally wonderful kiss.

Cassie took a step toward the door. "Thank you again," she said, in an obvious hint that it was time for Gene to be leaving.

"Cassie—"

Whatever else Gene was going to say was lost in a huge explosive sound louder than any of the previous thumps from the kitchen, followed by Dudley bounding into the living room, dragging his leash and the basement doorknob after him.

"Dudley, no," Cassie screamed.

Gene didn't scream, didn't make any movement at all. He simply sat frozen as the young dog leaped for his newest favorite chew-toy.

Thwump, went the couch as the dog landed next to Gene.

"Dudley," screamed Cassie as the doorknob on the end of the leash acted like a lasso, wrapping itself around her leg.

As the dog moved onto Gene's lap, the leash-tied Cassie fell onto both of them. Gene on the bottom, Dudley in the middle and Cassie on the top.

A mastiff sandwich.

"Help," screamed Gene, finally becoming unfrozen as Dudley once again began licking his face.

"I'm trying," screamed Cassie, trying to unwind the leash from her leg.

"What is going on in here?"

Cooper stood in the living room doorway surveying the scene.

"Woof," barked Dudley, giving up his favorite chew toy for his favorite friend.

"Help," yelled Cassie as she was helplessly dragged across the thankfully slippery hardwood floor after the dog.

"Dudley, sit." Again the dog obeyed Cooper's command, this time landing on Cassie.

"Oh, so it's you," Gene said, wiping his face with the afghan that covered the back of her couch—an afghan Cassie's Grandma Rose had made and given her as a sixteenth birthday present.

"Cut that out," she yelled at Gene.

He carelessly tossed the afghan aside and advanced on Cooper. "I should have known you wanted more than free meals all those nights you spent with Cassie."

"Maybe if you'd been around more, Cassie wouldn't have needed me for company."

"Hey, you two, remember me? The woman trapped under the dog?" She gave Dudley a push that didn't budge him the slightest bit.

"Cassie understood I was working overtime getting the company's books ready for the big audit."

"Maybe if you'd done your job right the first time there would have been nothing to get ready for the audit and you could have spent all those evenings with your fiancée, rather than at the office."

"Help," Cassie interjected, still trying to push the dog, but because he was on her legs, she had no leverage.

"Maybe if you had kept your lips off her, she'd have taken her engagement ring back."

"Maybe she wouldn't have liked my kiss so much if you'd taken care of her physical needs."

Cassie pushed against the dog, but wished she was pushing the two male heads together. "Maybe the only physical need *she* has right now is someone removing the puppy from her legs," she pleaded.

Cooper leaned down, grabbed Dudley's collar and physically moved the dog over.

"Sit," he commanded again. This time the puppy sat on the floor, much to Cassie's relief.

She untwisted the leash from her ankle and stood up. "Now, it's time for you two gentlemen to leave— no maybes about it. Cooper, didn't you say something about an early meeting tomorrow?"

He nodded, still eying Gene.

"And Gene, I know you're at the office no later than seven-thirty."

"I prefer working when it's quiet."

"Then, there you go. Good night, gentlemen. Gene, thank you for the proposal, but no thank you. And Cooper, thank you for riding to my rescue, but as you can see everything is fine."

"Aren't you going to thank him for the kiss?" Gene asked, sarcasm dripping from his tone as surely as slime had been dripping from his face a moment ago.

"That too, Coop. It was a nice kiss. Now, go. Both of you. Dudley's a growing puppy and needs his rest."

"He's growing?" Gene gasped.

"He'll probably end up weighing over two hundred pounds," Cooper said ever so helpfully.

Looking horrified at the mere thought, Gene backed up slowly, never taking his eyes off the dog who was still sitting patiently next to Cooper.

At the door he stopped. "Are you coming, Cooper?"

Ignoring Gene, Cooper said to Cassie, "Tomorrow we talk."

"Fine. Whatever. But tonight you both leave."

Sighing she shut the door. Dudley still sat where Cooper had left him. She walked over and unclasped the leash from his collar.

"What a mess," she groaned.

She wasn't sure if she was talking about Dudley, the slime factory masquerading as a dog, or the kitchen—whose damage she didn't even want to survey—or her heck-of-a-kissing neighbor, or lastly her ex-fiancé who wanted to re-fiancé her.

But whatever mess it was, she didn't want to try and figure it out tonight.

Chapter Five

"*H*i, you're on Night Calls with Cassie."

"Hi, Cassie. My name's Rhonda and I really hope your boss, Craig, picks me as his date. I was hoping you'd go to bat for me and convince him I'm the girl for him."

"Why do you think you're Miss Right?"

"Because I'm intelligent, even-tempered, and a good companion. That sounds like what he needs." She gave a nervous laugh. "I know, he could get a dog with all those qualities and not need the hassle of dating, but for me each date is exciting because with each new date there's a sense of hope and of possibilities. And from what you've said about your boss, he seems like he could use a bit of both . . ."

"Thanks, Rhonda, I'll make sure he sees your let-ter. And we have another caller who's interested in our Craig."

"Cassie, Craig needs to pick me for his date."

"What characteristics set you apart, caller."

"I've already got a wedding dress. Now, all I need is a groom . . ."

Cassie raced down a hall wearing a long wedding dress, opening door after door, looking for her wedding.

"Gene," she called, again and again, listening to her voice echo along with the beat of the doors slamming shut. She had to find him, had to find . . .

Cooper. Standing in a middle of a field, his arms extended, welcoming her into them. Still wearing her wedding dress, she walked toward Cooper, only to find Dudley was sitting on her dress's train. She pulled and pulled. Finally the thin fabric gave, and Cassie fell into his arms.

Then they were suddenly standing on her porch and Cooper was kissing her again. Holding her, closer, closer . . .

The alarm buzzed and Cassie awoke with a start from her dreams. Instead of finding Cooper in her arms, she found a snoring puppy.

"You're a bed hog," she mumbled as she tried to disentangle herself from a snoozing dog and blankets that were twisted around her.

Dudley lazily opened one eye as she finally wormed her way out of bed.

"Oh, go back to sleep. You can have the whole bed to yourself now." His eye promptly plopped shut and Dudley scooted over a bit to the right, taking up the space Cassie had vacated while she shuffled off to the kitchen.

A cup of hot green tea and some whole wheat toast with honey was her breakfast norm, but today it just didn't sound appealing. She wanted comfort food. After last night's fiasco, followed by dreams that left her feeling unsettled, Cassie deserved whatever comfort she could manage.

Ice cream.

Ice cream was just what she needed. It was a dairy product, so it was sort of healthy, she reasoned with herself, and yet decadent enough to make her feel better.

She opened the freezer, and after scanning the cartons decided death at the hands of chocolate was the way to go.

She grabbed the carton, opened the fridge and grabbed the chocolate sauce as well. Dipping a spoon straight into the ice cream carton, she drizzled the already oozing chocolate confection with even more of her liquid drug of choice. Maybe if she ate enough ice cream she could freeze her emotions.

Maybe the whole thing had been just another

series of odd dreams. Cooper's kiss, Gene's second proposal, Dudley . . . but one quick glance at the mutilated basement door assured her it all happened.

So now what?

She pondered the question as she ate another healthy bite of her ice cream.

As a woman who had decided to stay single and become a new millennium career woman, she had way too many men on her mind. There was her ex-fiancé who wanted to get re-engaged. Add to that her neighbor who she thought was her friend, but turned out to be a kissing fiend. And then there was Dudley, her slime factory, bed-hogging puppy who sat on people's legs and broke basement doors.

What a mess, both literally and figuratively.

The only thing good that had come out of the last twenty-four hours was her initial matchmaking success of Leo and Fran. She was sure they had hit it off, and she had a strong feeling that they weren't just destined for a casual dating relationship. No, there were definitely sparks flying there.

Dudley padded into the room, glanced at the basement door, and sank to the floor with a plop.

"Just what were you thinking last night?"

Dudley's head rose a fraction of an inch, and he cocked it to one side as if he was trying to figure out just what he'd been thinking.

Despite her annoyance at having to fix what had been, pre-Dudley, a perfectly good basement door,

Cassie couldn't help laughing. "You're a real doofus, you know that don't you?"

Taking her words as absolution from his basement door crimes, Dudley rose, walked across the floor and sat right next to her.

"At least your not sitting on me. Do you have to go out?"

Not really expecting an answer, Cassie drizzled some chocolate right into the ice cream container and took another bite.

"You want out?" Dudley raced for the door. Unable to brake in time, he thudded into it. "Doofus," she murmured affectionately and let him out.

Thank goodness her backyard was fenced and she didn't have to put him on a leash. After last night, she didn't imagine Cooper would really be inclined to help her with the puppy.

And after last night, she wasn't really inclined to ask.

Darned man. Kissing her, commenting on her sexy arms, making her dog sit on her, and then haunting her dreams.

No, she wasn't about to ask the man anything. If she was lucky, he'd stay at his house.

Leaving Dudley in the backyard she returned to her breakfast, such as it was, and came to a life-altering decision. Not only was she going to remain single, she was done with men altogether.

Well, not all men. She'd still deal with her male

callers. Most of them at least were sane. And even if they weren't, she didn't have to date them. She just listened to their problems and offered advice.

Cooper needed more than a radio talk show host to solve his problems. No wonder none of his dates panned out—what woman wanted to date a man who was always oohing and aahing over elbows?

Cassiopeia Grant, that's who.

She sighed and took the last bite of her mushy ice cream. For the first time in her life ice cream wasn't making her feel better.

What was she going to do about Jonathan "call-me-Cooper" Cooper?

What had he done?

Cooper wasn't in the best of moods as he met with one half of his newest clients the next afternoon.

"And then she tossed all my football trophies out the window. I didn't mind the clothes, they just needed washing, but you know a man's trophies are sacred, and so did she. She knows that football is my life . . ."

Cooper had always accused Cassie of losing everything, but last night he'd been the one who'd lost—lost his head. And he had no clue why.

Oh, he knew when it had started. The moment his cute, little, absentminded neighbor walked out of her bedroom morphed into some type of siren the night before. It was as if she had cast a spell on him.

That was probably it.

She talked about her feelings all the time. Those feelings and her belief in love had built her a solid following. According to her listeners, she was usually right with her advice. And she fixed up friends with an enormous success rate.

Magic.

That was as good an explanation as any he could come up with. She was probably practicing some type of magic, casting spells willy-nilly all over the place, making perfectly sane men get turned on by mere elbows.

Yep, that was the answer. Cassiopeia Grant was a witch who'd cast a spell on him, turning him from a logical lawyer into an elbow-crazed lunatic.

Yeah, and instead of a black cat as a familiar, she had a drooling dog.

"I don't see what the problem is. So I coached football all summer and forgot our anniversary. It was a big scrimmage . . ."

Well, Cassie wasn't going to catch Jonathan Cooper in her matrimonial spell. He was onto her and her magical ways. No more kissing, no more fantasies.

Cooper was happy being single. He loved his work, loved his house, loved his life just the way it was, thank you very much.

Cooper was going to pretend he was as absent-minded as Cassie and just forget that last night ever happened.

No more thoughts of his crazy, pixie-like neighbor. No way.

"And she says I ignore her during football season. What do you think?"

"Mr.—" Cooper glanced at the file, "Arch, I think you should have paid more attention to your wife than to football."

"What?" Arch said.

"I mean, she's your wife, and if she was feeling left out, then you should have figured out some way to fix it. Maybe you could get her interested in the game. Or maybe you could pay attention to her the rest of the week so that she doesn't mind when you take a few hours to watch a game."

"Listen, I came here for a divorce lawyer, not a therapist."

"Sorry," Cooper said, realizing what he'd just said to a client. "Uh, let's talk about what you want out of this divorce."

Montgomery Arch was a prime example of why Cooper should avoid the matchmaking antics of his neighbor. There was no such thing as love, despite her rose-colored vision of the world.

By the time he got home, he'd convinced himself that whatever had happened last night with Cassie was due to some kind of temporary insanity. He watched her and Dudley from his kitchen window after he got home. They were playing some odd sort of tug-of-war game with a baseball bat in Cassie's backyard. It looked like Dudley was winning the round, just as Cassie took a nosedive. Dudley dropped the bat and ran to Cassie, bent on reviving her with kisses.

"Get out of here, you goof," he heard her yell.

Would she yell the same thing at him if he dared venture over to her house? He probably deserved it if she did.

What had he been thinking last night? Where on earth did he ever get the elbow attraction? Cooper didn't have a clue, but whatever had been in the air last night was gone now.

He watched Cassie from the window, and didn't have the least bit of trouble looking at her elbows. Granted, they were an entire yard away, not sitting next to him in the car. But they were just fairly normal joints on fairly normal arms.

Cassie was once again just Cassie. His neighbor. His buddy. His chum. He was just going to forget all about that kiss last night, and of course if he forgot the kiss, he'd have to forget the dreams that had punctuated his sleep, sporadic at best, last night.

Now all he had to do was make sure Cassie forgot as well. And, given her gifted abilities in the forgetfulness department, that shouldn't be too much of a problem.

She'd probably already forgotten. All Cooper had

to do was pretend he had too—and then he'd have to work at making it the truth.

Yes, that was his plan. He'd just pretend last night hadn't happened and life could get back to normal.

Feeling better than he had all day, he headed over to her house.

Cassie saw Cooper's door open.

Get in your car and leave, she silently chanted.

Stay away.

You don't want to talk about last night.

It didn't look like any of her mental commands were making any difference. Cooper was making a beeline straight toward her.

She resigned herself to talking to her elbow-obsessed divorce lawyer neighbor when the knock on the door finally came.

"Ready to take Dud for a walk?" he asked.

Despite the fact Cooper avoided meeting her gaze, he seemed normal, at least the way the word *normal* was used relative to Cooper. No mention of last night's kiss or his sprint across over the hedge with the agility of an olympic hurdler, or even the slightest mention of Gene.

Just, *Ready to take Dud for a walk?*

Well, if he could ignore last night, Cassie certainly could too. She was willing to accept his arrival on her doorstep as a bid to move past last night's oddities. They'd ignore it, and they'd both forget all about dates and kisses and ex-fiancés.

"Let me get Dudley's leash."

Along with the leash she grabbed her sweatshirt. She might be willing to forget last night ever happened and she might want to keep Cooper as a friend, but there was no way was she exposing her elbows to him again, ever.

And it went without saying that she was never kissing him again either.

Ever.

Cassie tugged the sweatshirt over her head and pasted a smile on her face.

"Ready," she said with false brightness, hoping Cooper wouldn't notice just how forced her cheerfulness was.

"Hey, boy. How was your day?" Cooper asked, obviously not the least bit awkward around the dog.

Dudley's whole body was a giant wiggle as Cooper snapped the leash in place. "Are we heading anywhere in particular this evening?"

Dudley pranced to and fro, indicating he was ready to go anywhere, as long as they got started now.

"No place in particular. Just a nice quick walk to maybe work some of the excess energy out of Dudley." Cassie followed Cooper and Dudley as they headed up toward Thirty-eighth Street in unspoken agreement. "How about through the college campus?"

Mercyhurst College was only seven blocks away, and rather deserted during the summer. It was a beautiful place to walk.

Cooper nodded, and they walked in silence broken only by the occasional, "Dudley, heel."

The walk was mainly uphill and Cassie regretted the need to wear a sweatshirt. Sweat trickled in the most inconvenient places, making her itch like mad in areas she couldn't really scratch in public. She ran her hand over her forehead, at least able to dry that off a bit. Lucky for her it was only in the seventies. If it were any warmer she'd have collapsed by the time they crested the hill.

They reached Thirty-eighth Street and stood waiting for a break in the four lanes of traffic. Cassie was silently congratulating herself for not scratching under her breasts where pooling sweat was becoming an itchy temptation when Cooper blurted out, "About last night—"

"I don't want to talk about last night, I don't want to think about it, and goodness knows I don't want to dream about it." Cassie realized what she'd said and wished she'd learn to edit her words before saying them.

"Not that I dreamed about last night—" That was the truth, sort of. She hadn't replayed last night in her dreams. No, she'd created whole new fantasies featuring her and Cooper. Fantasies that involved more than kissing and had left her feeling rather . . . restless.

"Come on, let's go," she called, starting across the momentarily quiet four lane road.

Safely on the other side, she tried to extricate herself from the hole she'd dug. "I mean, I had a nice time on my date with *Leo,* but I don't think we'll be dating again. He and Fran are a definite match. So there is nothing to talk about."

Searching for anything to change the subject, she tried, "How was your day?"

Cooper gave the leash a tug when Dudley spent an inordinate amount of time exploring the scented wonders of a section of bushes.

"Come on, Dudley." He finally looked at Cassie, and totally ignored her question about work. "I wasn't talking about Leo or Fran."

"It doesn't matter. We're not talking about any aspect of last night. We're not even going to think about it. As far as we're both concerned, last night didn't happen. It's a temporal black hole, sucked completely out of our space-time continuum."

She hugged her sweatshirted arms to her chest, each hand clutching its opposite elbow. Though she might melt into a Wizard-of-Ozish puddle before she reached home, the baggy sweatshirt did a nice job of disguising the fact she had any body parts Cooper could notice.

"We're friends. And an easy friendship like ours is a rare thing. I don't want to ruin that."

"Cassie, I—"

"No, let me finish. We're friends, and that's all we can be. I was ready to settle for marriage-is-a-contract Gene, but I've learned my lesson. You would have thought, given my profession, I wouldn't have had to learn it at all, but I did and I have.

"My career is my new focus, but if I do ever date seriously, there are things I've learned. One is that casual dating is one thing, but even if I'm not looking to marry, I'm not willing to break my heart over someone who doesn't believe in love. I've seen how you are with women. After all, I've fixed you up on at least half a dozen dates since you moved in, and you've never dated a woman more than twice. You run away scared at the slightest hint of intimacy. Well, if I was going to have a relationship—which I won't—I'd want intimacy, lots and lots of intimacy."

She thought of Gene, and added, "And, I'd want a man who sparks more than a mild feeling of friendship. I want the whole works—passion, mixed with friendship. I'd want love and a family. I'd want a marriage that's more than a contract, but a lifelong love affair. Since I can't have any of that, I simply want to concentrate on my career. Maybe eventually I can have Night Calls syndicated. Wouldn't that be something? But in order for that to happen, I have to be totally focused on work."

Cassie had never really thought about syndication until the words tumbled out of her mouth, but she realized that might be just what she should focus on.

Advancing her career. It certainly was a better idea than finding true and everlasting love.

Dudley finished watering a signpost and shook his head, spraying spit in a three-foot radius.

"Dudley," Cassie yelled, dodging the biggest of the goobers.

Cooper wasn't as fast as she was, but didn't say a word as he rubbed a splotch of slime into his jeans.

Cassie's gaze couldn't help but stray to those nicely fitted jeans that so aptly emphasized the fact Cooper spent a lot of time outdoors, working hard, and toning . . . the area the jeans covered so nicely.

She had to get her mind back on straightening out their relationship, and off Cooper's backside. "Now, our kiss was nice," God forgive her for that understatement, she thought, "but I know it was just a heat of the moment sort of thing."

"An aberration," Cooper supplied a bit too hastily. Obviously he'd been having the same sort of thoughts Cassie was having.

"That's right. And, we're just going to forget that it ever happened and go back to being friends. Okay?"

Cooper realized he should be heaving a huge sigh of relief.

Cassie had just suggested exactly what he'd been thinking all day. Ignore whatever last night's aberration meant and go back to being friends. And yet, rather than relief he felt annoyance. "Fine."

"You don't seem fine." She studied him a moment. "You're not mad, are you?"

Mad?

He tugged on the dog's leash. That's all Cassie wanted him for, walking the dog. Not kissing. Not dating. He was just her friendly neighborhood dog-walker. "Why would I be mad?"

"I don't know. You're the one who ran away after our kiss. I thought you'd be relieved I wanted to forget about it. It was obviously a disappointing kiss for you."

"Yeah, you'd think I'd be relieved." He was relieved, wasn't he?

"Sure, sure I'm relieved," he said, more for his own benefit than Cassie's.

Friends.

"We're friends. I've never had a friend who was a woman before. I think that must be what happened last night. I mean, there you were, not looking a bit like my friend Cassie, but like some, well, some woman and there was your—"

"Let's forget the *and*," she said.

"Well, I was just unprepared for it," he continued. "When we went to dinner and it was obvious that Fran and Leo had hit it off, which means you and I were together—though we weren't really together— and I think my dating hormone took over."

"Dating hormone?"

"Yeah, it's the little hormone that kicks in when a man takes a woman out. It pushes him into making a move on her, whether he wants to or not."

"Whether he wants to or not?"

Cooper heard a certain dangerous note in Cassie's tone. Now what had he said?

She got mad when he kissed her, got mad when he apologized, and was mad now, and he didn't have a clue why. "Yes, whether he wants to or not. I mean, I didn't want to kiss you. But that dating hormone kicked in, and there it was."

"And this dating hormone. Does it kick in when you go out with your male friends?" Cassie asked.

"No. Of course not." They left the road behind and entered the college campus, walking along the boulevard that led to the beautiful brick main building.

"How about your other female friends? Do you go around kissing them?"

Dudley shook his head again, but this time they both managed to dodge the slimy spray.

"That's what I've been trying to tell you. I don't have any other female friends, so my poor dating hormone didn't quite know what to make of you. I mean, you have to admit, you didn't look like my pal Cassie last night."

Cassie stomped ahead, and suddenly whirled around. "What did I look like?"

"A woman, that's what. And I can tell you Cassie,

it was a bit unnerving. But, we're past it now. You're here tonight in your baggy jeans and ratty sweatshirt, and your hair, well, it looks like it normally does too, not all slicked back and fancy . . ."

He searched for a way to describe her hair last night. Her normally wild spikes had been smooth and he'd had the urge—an almost overwhelming urge—to reach over and tousle it into its slightly sexy normal disorder.

"And?"

"And tame like it did last night. I mean, I'm used to your wild hair," he didn't mention the word sexy, "not that sophisticated woman stuff you did with it last night."

Cassie stood silent, obviously absorbing what he'd said.

He'd done it, Cooper thought. He'd made her understand they were just buddies. Now, they could put last night's mistake behind them and just go on as friends. He'd walk Dudley for her, she'd cook an occasional meal for him and go back to setting him up with other women—women who didn't necessarily have wedding bells ringing in their ears.

Jonathan Cooper wasn't against dating, but he was only thirty-three and certainly not ready to settle down with any one woman. Not even a woman with the sexiest arms he'd ever seen.

Cassie's thoughtful expression disappeared and was replaced with a smile. Cooper breathed a sigh of relief. Yes, she understood. Things were back to normal.

"I can see you've given this a lot of thought." She started walking again along the path that was bordered by the dining hall on one side and a grassy grotto on the other.

"As soon as our lips touched, I knew it was wrong," Cooper said. "I mean, you and I, a couple? Come on."

Dudley stood, gazing longingly down the grassy hill. "You want to run, boy?"

Since the campus was deserted for the summer, Cooper clicked the leash off the puppy's collar, and laughed as Dudley tripped his way down the hill. "Come on back up here, you goof." Dudley happily obliged.

Yes, life was back in order.

Chapter Six

"*Hi, you've reached Night Calls.*"

"*Hi, Cassie. This is Matthew. My fiancée and I just broke up.*"

"*I'm sorry to hear that, Matthew.*"

"*My friends keep telling me I need to jump back into the dating scene, and since you just lost a fiancé as well, I thought maybe we could jump back in together at the Splash Bash . . .*"

Cassie watched Cooper as he jumped behind a tree in the college grotto, playing a cross between hide-and-seek and tag with Dudley.

It took awhile, but the puppy caught on and began chasing after Cooper, who dodged behind another tree, barely staying one step ahead of the dog.

It was a rather endearing sight that sort of made her heart melt. Or it would have if she wasn't already so hot—not because of her sweatshirt but out of annoyance at Cooper's obtuseness.

It wasn't that she wanted to be a couple with her insensitive neighbor—her buddy, her pal.

No. Cassie was content to be a matchmaking career woman who lived alone in blessed singleness with her drooling dog. It was just that even a career woman enjoyed some drooling from time to time of the undog variety.

Cooper's slight case of drooling last night was like a salve to her bruised ego, even if she wasn't interested in him in that way. But to have him tell her it was just some dating hormone kicked into overdrive—some mistake—was a direct attack on her fragile ego reserves.

So, oh yeah, she was hot, almost fuming at the insult.

Cassie pulled off the *ratty* sweatshirt that was making Cooper feel so complacent about his *pal* Cassie and knotted it around her waist. She was thankful she had a tank top underneath, a tight tank top.

"We'll just forget that kiss ever happened," Cooper continued as he leaned down and reattached Dudley's leash to his collar.

Forget it?

Okay, Cassie would learn to forget the kiss that

had haunted her dreams last night, but she was going to be darned sure Cooper never forgot. If she had her way, he would remember nothing else for some time to come.

"Maybe you can forget last night's kiss, but what are you going to about this one?" Even as she asked the question she made her move.

She stood on tiptoes in order to reach his lips and welcomed the remembered sense of rightness that accompanied kissing Cooper.

Confusing. Wonderful. Scary. Dazzling.

Part of Cassie wanted to stay like this—her lips pressed to Cooper's—forever. But the other part, the saner part, knew that she had to let go. Regretfully, she broke the contact.

Kissing Cooper might feel right, but it was wrong. They wanted different things. He wanted a good time, she wanted a relationship. He only saw the unhappy side of marriage—marriages that had ended—and Cassie still believed in love, believed there actually were happily-ever-afters.

There was no way to bridge those two opposite wants and beliefs in order to satisfy the pressing need of desire.

"I'm sorry," she whispered as she backed up. She needed some space, needed to get away from Cooper and his addictive kisses. "Listen, would you finish the walk with Dudley? I need to go home."

"Cassie—"

"Really, I just can't. Just drop Dudley off in the backyard when you're done."

This time it was Cassiopeia Grant who ran.

She ran home, forcing herself not to think about Jonathan Cooper and his very kissable lips. She wasn't going to think about how absolutely right it felt to kiss the man, because of course it was wrong.

The entire run home, Cassie concentrated on not thinking about Cooper. These feelings—feelings she refused to even try to define—were just illusions. She was just rebounding after her disastrous near marriage to Gene. The fact that Cooper lived next door made him a perfect target to rebound with.

Yes, that was it. She had kissed Cooper because of Gene, not because Cooper was so supremely kiss-able. They were just neighbors—friendly neighbors. Nothing more, nothing less. Cassie's unnamed feelings for Cooper and the two kisses they had shared were all Gene's fault.

She crossed another street and finally came to her own block. Home. She'd go home and she'd get herself under control. She would forget this nonsense with Cooper.

Actually, her original plan was best. She was going to forget men altogether and concentrate on her career.

Yeah.

She needed to concentrate on her callers because it

was becoming painfully obvious she was much better at fixing other people's love lives than fixing her own.

Before Gene there had been an embarrassing number of less-than-perfect relationships in her life. Then she'd thought she could form a lifelong, loving union with Gene, a man who merely saw marriage as a convenience, a contractual convenience. And now she was kissing her unmatchable neighbor.

The idea of becoming a single-minded career woman with a drippy dog suddenly held more appeal than ever.

She'd never have to worry about Dudley seeing their relationship as a contract, or even as a kissing relationship. Though he was young, the puppy must realize that with his drooling problem, kissing wasn't going to rank high in his future.

Home. Cassie sighed. She'd go eat some more ice cream, and get over this horrible week. She'd—

She spotted a car in the driveway. What was he doing here again? Before she did anything else, she was going to have to deal with contract-loving Gene first.

"Gene? Did you forget something last night?"

He was leaning against the hood of his car, arms folded across his chest, looking annoyed. "We never finished our discussion."

"I'm afraid we did." She started patting her jean's pockets, looking for her house key, praying she'd remembered to bring it along.

Gene's hand caught her wrist. "I don't think you understand. I'm willing to marry you."

"Unfortunately, I understand all too well. And, more unfortunately, I'm not willing to marry you. Ever." She yanked her wrist out of his hand. "And now, if you'll excuse me, I have work to do."

"Work?" Gene's eyes narrowed in suspicion. "Or do you have another date?"

Cassie had reached the conclusion that she had indeed forgotten her house key, and started toeing the gravel rocks that filled in under her bushes, looking for the key she thought she remembered hiding there.

"Really," she said, "it's none of your concern if I'm dating. I'm a free agent."

"How many men are you dating tonight?"

"Five. And that's before I leave for work."

She kicked a pile of rocks, not caring that Gene would discover her hiding place. She'd just find a better one after he left.

"Ten, even, if you count the guys I'm seeing after work. Maybe more. I'm thinking about trying for the Guinness World Record of dating the most men at one time. And even the station is trying to get in on it with the Date Cassie Contest. Now leave me alone."

"Whatever it is you're trying to prove, I've had enough of it. You'll take back your ring, we'll apply for a Pennsylvania marriage license since we won't be married in New York, and we'll be married as soon as we're able."

Where was that key? Cassie leaned down and dug with her fingers under the rocks, sure that she'd hidden a key here. Unfortunately, she'd hidden it so well, she couldn't find it.

Gene just continued talking, obviously enjoying the sound of his own voice and the fantasy he was weaving. ". . . I know we talked about living here after the wedding, but given the fact you're going around kissing your neighbors, I think it would be better if we moved into a new neighborhood."

"Kissing my *neighbor,* singular—not *neighbors.* And I'm not marrying you," Cassie growled.

Her fingers struck something that was non-rockish. The key? No, it was a very old soda tab. How many years had it been since they put tabs on soda cans?

"And, by next year we'll have the first of our three little Giffords, and of course he'll be a chip off the old block."

"And if it's a girl?" Cassie asked, momentarily stopping her key exploration in annoyance. The arrogance of the man, assuming he could control the gender of his children, and by his assumption, assuming that boys were more preferable than girls.

"It won't be. I bought a book on how to guarantee the gender. We'll have two boys, then a girl."

Children with Gene? At one point she must have known that if she married him she'd have to be intimate with him, and it must not have caused her much concern, but now Cassie couldn't imagine sharing a life and having children with the man. "And if the storks don't take orders from Gene Gifford, what then?"

Gene knelt down next to her. "Things will be perfect, you'll see that." He reached into his pocket and retrieved her engagement ring. "Now slip your ring back on your finger."

"I won't. Don't you see, Gene? This was never meant to be. You deserve someone who will love you to distraction, and so do I. Neither one of those people is either one of us, if you follow me . . ."

He still held her ring out, waiting for her to take it as he continued, "Of course, with all the kids to care for, you'll have to give up your job. It won't be good for the children if you spend your nights talking about romance on the radio."

"I wouldn't quit even if we were getting married, which we're not. I worked hard for my career, and it's going well. It's important to me, and to all the people I've helped. Even if we were getting married—which we're most definitely not—I wouldn't give up my work."

Cassie jumped to her feet. Forget the key, she was getting out of here.

Gene was on his feet as well, grabbing at her arm again. Cassie moved aside, unwilling to bear his touch.

"Cassie. Here's Dudley," Cooper called cheerful-ly, much too cheerfully.

Gene whirled. "You," he said with enough emo-tion in his tone to let both Cooper and Cassie know that being *you* wasn't a good thing.

"Gifford," Cooper said pleasantly.

There was a dangerous air about Cassie's previ-ously mild-mannered neighbor. She could see it as easily as she could see what a fool she'd been to ever think she loved Gene Gifford.

"Get that beast away from me," Gene hollered as Cooper and Dudley came closer.

The dog, spying last night's chew-toy, rushed to Gene's side and nuzzled his knee, leaving a glisten-ing trail in his wake.

"He likes you."

"I don't like him." Gene edged farther away, clos-er to the sidewalk. "Maybe Cooper will take him when you move out."

Cooper momentarily diverted his attention from Gene to Cassie. "You're moving?"

"No." Her life might be chaos at the moment, but she wasn't going anywhere. This was her home. Grandma Rose had left the house to her, and she was staying put. No, she wasn't leaving home, especially with Gene, that much she was sure of.

"Yes," Gene corrected her. "We're getting a place away from this neighborhood and away from you. I can't have you kissing my wife."

"I'm not going to be your wife," Cassie reminded her ex-fiancé, emphasizing the *ex* in her mind.

"Tonight I wasn't the one kissing your wife—"

"*Ex*-fiancé," Cassie corrected.

"Ex-fiancé," Cooper echoed obligingly. "No, I wasn't the one doing the kissing, Cassie was."

"You kissed Cooper tonight?" Gene asked weakly.

"Just a little," Cassie admitted, "because I was sweaty and that was all Cooper's fault. He said he was my buddy and that he was going to forget I had elbows, and of course he could forget I had them since I'd covered them with the sweatshirt, which is why I was sweaty and hot. So I took off the sweatshirt then I kissed him, just to remind him that I have elbows."

To Cooper she added, "The elbow thing is a little creepy."

"Cooper knowing you have elbows is creepy?" Gene asked, edging closer.

"Yeah." Cassie couldn't help but glance at the body parts in question. Ordinary, common-looking elbows. She waved them toward Gene. "I mean, they're just elbows, nothing special."

"So you kissed him?" Gene took another step closer.

"They're nice elbows," Cooper protested.

"They're just a normal piece of anatomy," Cassie corrected. "But though my elbows might not be anything special, my kisses are unforgettable, or at least they should be."

"I didn't say I forgot, I just said we *should* forget," Cooper said at the same time Gene said, "I never thought about it before, but your kisses are quite forgettable. I mean, I can't remember the last time we kissed."

Cassie chose to ignore Cooper and concentrate on Gene. She wasn't sure if he was talking about her kisses or elbows, but she didn't really care. "My kisses are quite special, at least when I'm kissing Cooper."

Oh, wrong thing to say. Cooper wanted to forget the kisses.

"And maybe you're right. Since I kissed Cooper, I can't even remember what your kisses are like. That's another reason why we're not getting married. I mean, a wife should think her husband's kisses unforgettable, shouldn't she?"

Gene closed what little gap remained between them and grabbed Cassie. "Let's see if you can forget this."

Gene Gifford, the contract-loving accountant was going to kiss her.

Yes, Gene was going to kiss her, and then Cooper would kill Gene. Cassie could see the kiss in her ex-fiancé's eyes, just as easily as she could Cooper's willingness to maim the man in his eyes.

Since Gene was right in front of her, she couldn't see Cooper, but she could sense his presence and knew that Gene's lips would never reach hers.

But before Cassie could break off the attempted kiss, or the attempted murder, Dudley took action.

Cassie and Cooper might not like Gene's kisses, but Dudley did. And since Gene had so obligingly come back into reach, the puppy jumped up and placed a very enthusiastic puppy kiss on Gene's chin, which was as high as his tongue could reach.

"Gross," Gene shouted.

Obviously forgetting he was going to defend Cassie's virtue by killing Gene, Cooper laughed. "Now *there's* a kiss no one could forget," he roared.

Cassie wanted to be insulted. After all, Cooper had kissed her twice. Okay, he hadn't really kissed her twice—he'd kissed her once and been kissed by her once. Either way, he should defend her honor, instead he was laughing like a lunatic as Dudley tried to reach Gene—who had backed out of reach—for a repeat performance.

"Get that beast away from me," the slightly slimed Gene hollered.

Cooper obliged and reigned Dudley in enough to prevent the dog from kissing Gene, but not enough to allow Gene from reaching Cassie. "Just take that mutant mutt to your house, and let Cassie and me finish this discussion."

"We're finished, Gene. I'm so sorry, but I don't want to marry you. I don't want to kiss you. And I don't really even want to see you again."

"You'll regret this Cassie," Gene promised.

"No, Gene, I'll forget this. Now, if you'll pardon me, I have to dig up my house key," Cassie said, hoping she'd laced enough finality into her tone to rid herself of her ex-fiancé for good.

"Cassie," Gene started.

"You heard the lady, Gifford. Good-bye." Cooper let some slack into Dudley's leash, allowing the dog to leap within inches of Gene.

Sensing defeat, or possibly fearing more slime, Gene Gifford, the forgotten, unlamented ex-fiancé, left.

"Well, that's that," Cassie said as she watched Gene's very proper, reliable black Lincoln pull away from the curb. "I hope we've seen the last of him." She turned to Cooper. "Thank you for the help. I could have handled Gene, but I'm not too proud to appreciate the assistance."

She held her hand out and Cooper silently handed her Dudley's leash. The dog sat on his haunches with a plop. "Come on, Dudley. We'll go around back." She pulled at the leash, anxious to get away from Cooper who was probably staring at her overexposed elbows. "Come on, Dudley, you dud."

The dog sat perfectly still, as if his butt had been superglued to the cement walk.

"Let me." Cooper took back the leash. "Unlock the door, and I'll let him in for you, and then we'll talk."

"I can't find my key, but don't let that worry you.

I'll take care of it, and I'll take care of my own dog, thank you." She opened the gate to the fence. Cooper walked through it and unhooked Dudley' leash.

"Thank you," Cassie said, taking the leash. "You can leave now. I don't want to talk to you. As a matter of fact, I'm done talking to you."

There, she'd told him. Cassie went to slam the gate in his face, but unfortunately it wouldn't close because of the size eleven sneaker that was wedged between the gate and the fence.

"Move your foot," she said.

"I thought you were done talking to me," Cooper taunted, wedging his great big, sneaker farther into the space.

"I am done talking to you, at least I am if I can get you to move your foot out of my way."

Cooper's foot didn't budge, but his lips did, into what might appear to be a smile to the casual observer. "Maybe you're done talking to me, but I can assure you that you're not done kissing me."

"Oh, yes, I'm done with that too."

Cassie stomped on the huge target Cooper's shoe presented, but he didn't move an inch.

"I only kissed you because I didn't like you saying you could forget my kisses. No woman wants to think her kisses are forgettable."

"Ah, but you want Gene to forget your kisses. Why not me?"

He had her there, darn it.

Cassie frowned at the flaw in her logic. She wasn't sure how to remedy the contradiction.

"I don't know," she finally said. "And I don't want to know. I'm done with men. After all the calls I've taken from them, I thought I understood them, but I don't. You're a bunch of contradictory Y chromosomes and I'm absolutely done with the entire race."

"Gender."

"What?"

"Men are a gender, not a race."

"That too. Now, go away." She tried to slam the gate on Cooper's shoe, hoping he'd jump back and she could close it, but the foot, and Cooper, remained firm.

"Cassie, our fighting is upsetting Dudley."

The dog was lying on the ground whimpering.

"He'll get over it as soon as we're done discussing men. Discussing, not fighting. And we're done now, so Dudley's life is looking great."

"We're not done." Blatantly switching topics, he asked, "And how are you going to get into the house?"

"I'll probably have to climb through the dining room window again."

"Want a boost?"

Cassie's first impulse was to say yes. After all, her dining room window was high enough to be difficult to crawl through. Last time she'd had to drag the picnic table from the center of the yard to the window.

Cooper's boost would making breaking into her house easier.

But in order to help her, he'd have to come into her yard and touch her. Yeah, there was no way he was going to be able to boost her through the window without at least some minimal touching.

Touching Cooper wasn't a good idea.

"Cassie, I just asked if you wanted help getting through your dining room window, nothing more."

She swallowed convulsively. His second suggestion would involve a lot more touching and sounded even more appealing than the boosting, but she knew it was a bad idea.

A very bad idea.

"Come in," she croaked, releasing the gate so more than just his foot could enter the yard. "But we're going to do it with a minimum of touching."

"You're sure about that?"

"Oh, yes I'm sure."

Sighing the sigh of a man exhausted by too many trials and tribulations, Cooper trailed after Cassie to the window.

"It's not all that hard," she said. "If you give me a boost, I just have to push up the screen and crawl in. Can you manage it?"

He snorted in a way that said he was insulted as well as felt put-upon by his troublesome neighbor.

Well, let him snort. As long as he was annoyed he wasn't thinking about her elbows. Thank goodness he wouldn't have to go near them to boost her through the window.

He cupped his hands.

She placed her foot in it.

He boosted.

Yes, this was going to work just fine, she thought as she pushed up the screen and lifted her left leg to put it through the window.

Dudley barked. Rather than continuing into the window, Cassie glanced down in time to see the puppy jump at Cooper's back.

"Dudley, no," she shouted.

Cooper teetered a second with Cassie's foot still in his hands, Dudley's paws on his back.

Dudley was the first to topple. The loss of the dog's weight set Cooper even more off-balance.

Teeter, totter.

Cooper fell backward, and since Cassie didn't have enough of her body through the window to out-weigh the part that was still outside the window, and given that she didn't have the power of levitation, she fell down, right on top of the puppy and her annoying elbow-lusting neighbor.

From the middle of the pile, Cooper said, "Since we're here on the grass together, maybe it's time to try some more of that kissing?"

Kissing Cooper again would be a mistake. A humongous mistake.

Cassie tried to tell herself this, but his lips were

just a fraction of an inch away from hers and the distance was easily bridgeable; as easily as her common sense was ignored.

Despite her misgivings, her lips met his with an uncharacteristic eagerness.

Here, their bodies both seemed to say, *here is where we belong*.

Cassie forgot she was lying on Cooper, that it was broad daylight and they were in her backyard easily viewed by at least half a dozen neighbors. All she remembered was that anywhere with this man was where she belonged.

Suddenly he drew back and loosened his grip. "Cassie, we really do need to talk."

Common sense came flooding back like water escaping a broken dam. Cassie rolled off Cooper and tried to pull herself back together. "I think we need to stop kissing more than we need to talk. We seem to talk about talking a lot, and all we end up doing is kissing."

"We need to talk about the kissing."

"No. We simply need to stop the kissing." She scrambled to her feet and walked back to the window. "And we can stop the kissing and talking as soon as I'm in my house."

Cooper rose.

"Dudley, sit," he commanded the puppy who obeyed him instantly.

"Here you go." He offered her his cupped hands and Cassie put her foot into them again and scrambled through the window as quickly as possible.

"Just shut the gate door on your way out. I'll let Dudley in later," she said as she slammed the window back into place and disappeared into the house.

What had she done? Kissed Cooper, that's what. And not just once, but twice. Twice in one night she'd kissed her antimarriage neighbor.

Well, there wouldn't be a third time. She was really done with men now.

She looked at the clock and realized she couldn't be done with men. She had to leave for work soon, and there was that whole date Cassie, Splash Bash contest to deal with.

A lot of nice letters, e-mails, faxes and calls had come through, for both herself and Craig. But Cassie couldn't seem to work up the least little bit of interest in any of them. The only man she wanted was the one she shouldn't want.

Dudley scratched at the back door.

Cassie checked that Cooper had indeed left before she let the puppy in.

"What a mess, Dudley. Talking, kissing, elbows, ex-fiancés, contests. . . . What happened to my simple life?"

Dudley whined his support and she leaned down and hugged him. "Thanks."

The only good thing that had come out of the last week was her dog.

"Just you and me, Dudley. That's how it's going to be."

He gave her a look of disbelief.

"Traitor."

Chapter Seven

"Hi, Cassie. Your station manager, Craig, might sound nice, but I don't want to enter any contest for some blind date. I want a man and I want him now. I'm tired of playing games, going on blind dates, hanging out at bars. Where can I meet a potential Mr. Right?"

"Mr. Right could be anywhere. At our Splash Bash, at your local church, at work, at the grocery store. Heck, Mr. Right could be right under your nose. You just have to be open to the possibility."

While the music played, Cassie thumbed through a bunch of entries for her blind date. Not one sparked any kind of interest. Oh, some sounded like nice

enough guys, but she didn't want a nice guy. She
wanted—

The door to her small studio opened. "Cassie, this
is ridiculous," Craig said, tossing a stack of letters on
the desk. "How am I supposed to pick a date from
this?"

She tossed her own pile of e-mails and letters next
to his. "I could ask you the same question. And let
me remind you, this was your idea."

"No. It was Ted's idea. We had such a spike in ratings last year with the Pickup Lines Contest, then
Ethan and Mary's wedding, followed by Punch and
Judy's wedding at the first Splash Bash, he thought
another contest would be perfect. A contest involv-
ing you, not me."

"Hey, I warned you when you forced me into it
that you'd regret it."

He slumped into a vacant chair across from her.
"Well, you were right, I do regret it."

"Hold onto that thought and let me take this call."
She picked up line one. "Hi, you've reached Night
Calls, here at WLVH where love is more than just a
song."

"Hi, Cassie. This is Melody. I'm faxing you a letter as soon as I'm off the phone. I'm hoping to win
a date with Craig."

"It just so happens that Craig's visiting me here in
the studio tonight. We were both looking through all
the wonderful letters that listeners have sent in," Craig

rolled his eyes and despite her own frustration, Cassie grinned, "and we're stumped as to how to narrow it down and pick a date. Any suggestions, Melody?"

Craig had stopped rolling his eyes and moved right onto shooting eye-daggers at her, which made Cassie's smile move from a small grin to a great big one. Making Craig mad was becoming the highlight of her night.

"I guess," Melody said slowly, "there's no logical way to pick a date."

"Because there's no logic to love, is there?"

"You're right. Just tell Craig, I hope he'll give me a shot. Could you play 'Desperado' for me?"

"I will. Thanks for calling, Melody."

She signed off and started editing the recorded call to play the next break.

"Was she suggesting I'm desperate?" Craig asked.

"I don't think so. I think she was suggesting it was time for you get off your high horse and let someone love you."

"Ha. She thinks I'm desperate. All the available women in Erie think that, thanks to you and this stupid contest."

"No, not all of Erie. Only our listeners. Of course, according to Ted, our listener base is growing. And again, I'll point out this was not my idea. You're mad at Ted, not me."

"I think the next WLVH contest is going to feature Ted Hyatt in some horrible, date type of way."

Cassie grinned. "I like the way you think. Maybe a holiday contest? Something that involves him and mistletoe. Lots of mistletoe."

"You're a devious sort of woman, Cassiopeia Grant."

She played Melody's recording and then put on 'Desperado' before taking another call.

"Hello, this is Cassie on Night Calls."

"Hi, Cassie."

She frowned. The voice sounded strangely familiar. Why was Cooper calling her?

"What can I do for you tonight, *caller*?"

"I'm calling for a bit of advice. You see, I have this friend. This very good friend. But suddenly things have changed, and I don't know what to do about it, but I do know I don't want to lose her friendship."

"So unchange things."

"I don't know if I want to do that either. We're good friends, and we've discovered we're also good kissers. The problem is, she's got this fairy tale idea of what love is. I don't think I could ever live up to her expectations of a Prince Charming. And to be honest, I don't know if I'd want to."

"Maybe you're wrong about what she's looking for. She might have given up on Prince Charming and decided to become a single career woman."

"That's what she says, but I don't buy it. She's the

type of woman who's destined to be married, to be in a long-term, ever-after sort of relationship."

"But you're not?"

"Oh, no, I fully expect to be married someday, but in a realistic, logical sort of relationship she'd never consider."

A wave of sadness swept over her. Cooper was right. They both wanted very different things from a relationship—not that she was looking for a relationship. She was a career woman now. A career woman with a huge, slimy dog.

"Have you been listening to my show? The last caller and I decided love isn't ever logical."

"Ah, but I don't believe in love. Sexual chemistry, compatibility, yes. Friendship even. But not a fairy tale sort of true love. So what do I do?"

She sighed. "It sounds like the two of you are too different to ever make anything work, so I'd back off and go back to just being friends." She paused and added softly, "That means no more kisses, no more talk of elbows. Friends."

"Yeah, that's what I figured." Cooper didn't sound any more enthused than she felt. "Well, thanks for the advice."

"Anytime, *caller.*"

"What was that?" Craig asked as she hung up. "Elbows?"

"Some men find elbows very appealing."

He shook his head. "All the weirdos come out at night and call you." He stood. "Elbows?" He shook his head again and started to walk out of the booth.

"Hey, don't forget your letters," Cassie called, before he could make his escape.

Craig shot her a disgruntled look as he turned around and took the pile. "Start thinking of what we're going to do to Ted."

"I will."

He shut the door and Cassie looked at her pile of letters. She just needed to find someone for a simple date. Career women dated, after all.

She tried to visualize the type of man Cassiopeia Grant, career woman extraordinaire should date.

Unfortunately, jaded, marriage-should-be-logical Jonathan Cooper was the only man she could think of.

Sunday the station's receptionist, Paula, had stopped in at Cassie's for coffee. She was a casual friend who had decided that since Cassie's show centered on love, Cassie was the perfect friend to talk to whenever she had man troubles. And Paula had a lot of man problems.

Today, Cassie had welcomed the distraction.

"Another disastrous relationship," Paula said. "It's not like I'm asking for a lifetime guarantee. I just want a man . . ."

"What are you looking for in a man?"

Cassie didn't want to look for a man herself. She'd

spent the morning going over the contest entries rather than the Sunday paper. Finding a date for the Splash Bash was looking for a needle in a haystack.

The pretty brunette's brow puckered in concentration. Lost in thought, she gazed out Cassie's kitchen window.

"I want . . ." Paula paused a moment, and then turned and smiled at Cassie. "I want him."

She pointed.

Cassie's gaze followed the direction Paula pointed at and she stifled a groan.

"Oh, Cassie, he's eye candy. And right now, I want something sweet. Is he taken?" Paula pressed.

Cassie watched Cooper carry a bag of groceries into his house. Taken? Jonathan Cooper? That would be the day. And if he ever was taken, it wouldn't be by Cassie. They'd settled that on the radio.

"No."

Paula's face brightened, but Cassie held her hand up and continued rapidly. "No, Cooper's not taken, and it's highly unlikely he'll be taken any time in the near future. He has commitment issues."

Cassie wasn't sure she was being exactly truthful. Cooper had never said he had commitment issues, he just didn't want to commit—at least not to any of the women she'd fixed him up with.

To be brutally honest, he might have fussed about those other blind dates, but he'd never made quite the commotion he'd made with her about their kisses.

He'd made it abundantly clear that the thought of dating, or kissing, Cassie was absolutely out of the question.

"Just because he hasn't committed to any woman in the past, doesn't mean he never will," Paula said slowly.

"And it doesn't mean he ever will, either."

"Do you think you could fix us up? I really need to go out with someone who will make me forget all about—" she cut herself off. "No, no, I'm not even saying his name. I've already forgotten it."

"I don't know if setting you up with Cooper will be possible."

Possible, but for Cassie not probable. To set Cooper up she'd have to talk to Cooper, something she should probably avoid for a while, at least until this brief rebound infatuation died down.

"You see, I've set Cooper up in the past, but . . ."

"But?" Paula tapped her fingernails on the kitchen table.

Bright red nails. Blood red. Darn, those were scary nails. Normally Paula's nails didn't catch her eye, but today they looked, well, intimidating.

Maybe if he went out with the perpetually perky Paula, he'd find Paula's elbows were even nicer than her own. Or, maybe he had a thing for blood-red vampire nails. Maybe he'd want to kiss Paula, and forget all about kissing Cassie.

The thought didn't sit well with Cassie and she

couldn't understand why. Cooper had made his opinion of the two of them as a couple absolutely clear. And of course Cassie agreed.

She did agree, right?

So setting Paula and Cooper up should be no problem.

"I could try," she offered without much enthusiasm. "I mean, maybe he'd want to go out with you."

"Oh, that would be lovely." The tapping increased in tempo. "Want to fill me in on him?"

"There's not much to say," Cassie said, continuing the train of thought internally, *Other than stop that infernal tapping.* "Cooper's self-employed."

No lie there.

"Is that another way to say he doesn't work?" The tapping slowed and Paula frowned, causing little tiny wrinkles to appear around her eyes.

"Well, he doesn't work much." Cassie knew she was skirting the truth and felt a small pang of guilt that evaporated as quickly as it came.

She racked her brain for something else to share with Paula. "And he can't cook."

"No?" Rather than intensify, the frown relaxed into an almost neutral expression.

"No." Cassie tried to make not cooking sound worse. "He's always over here looking for a free meal."

"Maybe it's not that he can't cook, maybe since he's self-employed he doesn't have money to buy food." The frown totally disappeared, replaced by a look of concern, which cleared just as quickly as Paula said, "He must have some money, he just took a bag of groceries into the house."

"That, that could be from the food bank. They have to put the free food in something. And look at his truck. It's seen better days."

Cassie knew Cooper rode the four-wheel drive truck hard, but she also knew about his pristine Mustang parked out of sight in his garage.

She glanced across the table at Paula. Maybe she'd gone too far. "I didn't mean to make it sound like he's destitute. I don't think that's an accurate description of his financial situation."

"Anything else I should know?" Paula asked neutrally.

"You still want me to fix you up with him?"

"Yes. I cook, and when I graduate, I'll be making good money. I'd complement him. Maybe we'd mesh. That's what I want, a logical relationship . . ." she let the sentence fade.

Logic. Love wasn't logical, but maybe a relationship could be. Yes, Cooper would probably love Paula with her blood-red, vampire nails.

Was there anything else Cassie should tell Paula about Cooper? She could mention that he kissed like . . . well, like no one she'd ever kissed before. Or that he was funny, and that he liked ice cream and drooly dogs. She could tell Paula any of that, but she didn't. "Let me see what I can set up with Cooper, and with a couple other men I think might hit it off with you."

"Have I mentioned lately you're a good friend? And I'm sorry about your wedding. I know that your show is built on this romantic idea of love, but maybe it's time to talk about something more realistic. Companionship, chemistry . . ."

"Going into a business deal? A contract?" Cassie asked, thinking of Gene.

"Yes. Who knows, maybe your neighbor will be my Mr. Compatible. Even if not, he's hot. And that's enough for now."

Paula was practically drooling over Cooper.

How would he feel about being wanted only for his looks? Knowing Cooper, he'd probably love being wanted on a physical level.

Cassie saw Paula out with a sigh of relief.

He'd probably feel complimented, Cassie continued her musing, still thinking about Cooper dating Paula later that evening. She'd been watching the clock, wondering if Cooper would show up to walk the dog.

"What do you think, Dudley?" she asked.

Dudley's tail wagged lazily.

"I don't know what to think," she confessed and put the last few dishes in the dishwasher. "One moment I want to run right into his arms and the next minute I want to run, just run, as far away as I can get.

"One minute I think I'd be happy concentrating on my career, and the next . . . well, all I can think about is Cooper."

She stroked the big puppy's head. "I don't think I've ever been so confused."

Once upon a time, she'd known what she wanted and what she was going to do with her life.

Professionally, she wanted to see her show continue to climb in the ratings. Maybe even be syndicated someday.

On a personal note she'd wanted love, and from that she'd build a family, a whole passel of kids . . . what she had planned to do with Gene.

Maybe that had been the problem. Gene always came last in her calculations. He should have come first if she loved him, which she hadn't, and which is probably why he came as an afterthought.

She filled the dishwasher's cup with soap and started it. Not knowing what other busy work she could find, Cassie simply sat down and stared out the window. It wasn't her fault the window faced Cooper's house. It wasn't as if she was waiting for him. No, not at all.

She wasn't thinking about Cooper at all. She was thinking about Gene and how she'd never loved him. That was about the only certainty in her life. She didn't love Gene—never had, never would.

She could simply fix Cooper up with Paula and

forget about him. Maybe if he began dating someone else things would get back to normal.

She had no claims on Jonathan Cooper, there was no reason why she shouldn't set Paula and Cooper up. Why, she'd only kissed the man three times. So, why did she get such a queasy feeling when she thought about fixing Paula up with Cooper?

She tried to sort out her feelings. Though they seemed to be bouncing all over the place like ping pong balls, there seemed to be a bit more bouncing toward wanting him. Could her feelings for Cooper be more than a combination of rebounding and friendship?

As if on cue, Cooper's front door opened and he emerged, heading over the hedge.

If they were only friends and a rebound attraction then why did her heart give this funny little flip just because he was coming over?

There could only be one excuse for queasiness and heart-flipping. The thought hit her like a ton of . . . mastiffs.

There was only one reason she was acting like this about Cooper. She'd worked on Night Calls for six years. She should have recognized the symptoms sooner.

Cassiopeia Grant, a woman who had built her career on love, was falling in love with her commitmentphobic, elbow-infatuated, divorce lawyer neighbor.

"I'm falling in love with him," she said aloud.

Dudley gave a little yap, as if to say he'd known it all along. Well, she hadn't known it.

She felt giddy with happiness. She was falling for Cooper.

On the heels of that thought, her heart thudded. But what if her feelings weren't genuine? She'd obviously been wrong about her feelings for Gene. How could she trust her feelings for Cooper?

She liked Cooper. Had liked him from the first day. Sharing meals and talking, just talking with no pressure—she was engaged so neither of them had any worries of sexual tension—every moment spent with Cooper had been a pleasure.

She heard him knocking on the door.

Part of her wanted to run, throw the door open, and throw herself into his arms. Instead she sat another moment at the table. Cooper might have kissed her, or been kissed by her, but he'd never indicated their relationship should move beyond friendship. As a matter of fact, he'd done his best to point out why it shouldn't.

Of course, so had she, and it turned out that she was falling for him—at least she thought she was.

"Come on, Cassie," she heard him call as he pressed the buzzer.

"How am I going to handle this?" she muttered to Dudley, who was already bounding for the front door.

Cassiopeia Grant had found a man to love, but from all indications, he didn't return her feelings, and never would. He wanted logic and compatibility. A mature, businesslike relationship.

Cassie didn't want that.

The big problem at the moment was that she didn't have a clue what she wanted.

So, now what?

Chapter Eight

"*This is Cassiopeia Grant at Night Calls. Tonight, I'd like to talk about hiding. Hiding from your feelings. Hiding from love . . .*"

Cooper pressed the doorbell again. He knew Cassie was in there. Did she think she could hide from what had happened? He'd thought his call to the station had been brilliant. They'd finally talked, and seemingly solved things.

Friends.

That's what they'd been.

That's what they were.

Saying so had sounded good last night.

Even today.

But here she was, hiding. And, as he spent the day destroying his practice, he'd found the word *friend* more and more distasteful.

Oh, yeah, it was all Cassie's fault that he was decimating his client base, slowly but surely.

He'd tried to talk three other clients into giving their marriages another try before going through with a divorce. Three potential clients who'd left his office, unsure whether they needed a divorce lawyer after all.

After each left, he'd sat and thought.

Thinking. It's all he'd been doing lately. He'd hoped talking would stop the thinking, but it had only made it worse.

He'd thought about Cassie, about kissing Cassie. He'd thought about being friends with Cassie. Heck, he'd even thought about talking to Cassie.

With all those thoughts, he would have hoped he had some idea what to do next, but fact was, he didn't have a clue.

Cassie had set him up on dates since he moved in, but not one of the women she'd set him up with had ever occupied his thoughts like Cassie was doing right now. None of the women he'd dated on his own had either. That particular thought was telling, but Cooper wasn't sure he was happy with what it was telling him.

They were friends.

At least they had been friends until her engagement with Gene Gifford had fallen through.

Gene Gifford.

This strange situation was all Gifford's fault.

Up until the moment he'd left the picture, Cooper had been free to enjoy Cassie's company, and he'd never given a thought to her elbows or her kisses. Now they were all he could think of.

Cassiopeia Grant. His cheerful little romantic. A woman who didn't just want to date a man, but who wanted a fairy tale romance, a romance that would end with the words "till death do us part." These words scared him to death.

Death do us part. Promising to love someone that long, with no contingency clauses, no built-in exceptions. It sounded so final. Cooper knew the phrase should be, "till we get tired of each other.

Commitment was just a condition of convenience. When it was no longer convenient to commit, all those fairy tale romance couples came to his office committed to ending their "lifelong" vows.

He realized he was still thudding rhythmically on Cassie's front door as it flew open. "Yes?"

No easy smile.

No, *Cooper, how nice to see you.*

Even if she'd said the words, Cooper wouldn't have believed she meant them, not with that ridiculous sweatshirt covering her elbows, and the look of suspicion in her eyes.

Did she think he was going to grab her and kiss her right her on her doorway?

The thought had merit.

"Yes?" she said again.

He had to pull himself together. Get things back on an even keel.

"Ready to take Dudley for a walk?" he asked, hoping his voice and expression betrayed none of his wayward thoughts.

"Wouldn't you prefer taking him yourself?"

"No." Why had he said that? Of course he'd rather take the dog for a walk by himself. Dudley didn't haunt him the way the puppy's perky owner did. "Would you prefer me taking him myself?"

"No." Her expression softened. "Of course not. Why should I?"

"I don't know, but you don't seem all that enthused to see me."

"I . . ." she hesitated a moment, then said, "I needed to talk to you anyway. Not about what we've been needing to talk about so frequently lately, because we're done talking about that. We settled all that on the radio. That was very clever, actually. Talking in a forum like that, over a phone line. It was easier, and goodness knows you like things easy in relationships, not that we have one. I mean, we agreed—"

"Breathe, Cassie," he said. "You're going to run out of oxygen with all your babbling. And I tell you, if you pass out, I'll let Dudley revive you."

The puppy was dancing around behind Cassie, anxious for his walk.

"Anyway, I don't want to talk about any of that anymore. Not ever again. Tonight, it's about something else. Something unrelated and—"

"Do you want to just tell me about while we walk?"

Talking with her about something unrelated to their recent conversations was good. It was what they used to do when they were merely friends and neighbors.

Cassie nodded. "Let me get Dudley's leash."

"Hey, Dud," Cooper said as he patted the sloppy puppy's giant head. "How're things?"

Dud looked up at Cooper, his droopy eyes looking sad. "That bad, huh?"

"What's that bad?" Cassie asked.

Cooper took the leash and clipped it onto Dudley's collar. "Nothing."

They walked half a block in silence.

"Cassie, about—"

"There's a woman who wants to meet you," she filled in before he could go any further. "Her name's Paula." No pause, not even for a breath, she started rattling off on another babble run. "She's the receptionist at the station. Smart and sexy, well, except for that nail thing."

"Nail thing?"

"Nothing." She shook her head and ran her fingers through her spiky hair. "I was wondering," Cassie continued, "if you might want to, well, if you want to take her out."

After what they'd been through the last few days, Cassie was still trying to fix him up? Cooper's first inclination was to say, *hell no, the only woman I want to date is you.* But somewhere between his thoughts and his mouth it came out as, "Sure," instead. That one word just blurted out before he stop it.

"Sure?" Cassie sounded surprised.

"Sure. I mean, we settled whatever our little relationship aberration was during our phone conversation, so there's no reason why I shouldn't take this woman out, is there?" He waited, oddly enough hoping she'd say, *yes, there is a reason. You and I have something going here.*

Slowly, she shook her head. "No, of course not. Paula will be delighted."

"I'm glad." Dudley paused to explore a forsythia bush. Cooper might have given him a few minutes, but he was anxious for this walk to be over. "Come on, Dud."

"Paula spotted you taking your groceries in today."

"That's nice." Whatever was happening between them obviously wasn't affecting Cassie the way it was affecting him.

"Paula only wants to date you because she thought you were cute."

"That's fine." Cassie saw him as her ace-in-the-hole, someone to foist on unsuspecting friends.

Yeah, he bet she didn't tell this new woman that he was a nonromantic, logic-loving lawyer.

"You're just a boy toy to her."

"Fine." A boy toy. That's all he was to Cassie. Someone to play with and then share with all her friends.

"Leo said he hated feeling like a piece of meat."

"That's Leo. I prefer women just want me for my body, rather than wanting . . ." his voice trailed off.

What did he want a woman to want from him?

"Rather than wanting what, Cooper?"

"I'd rather women were interested in the physical side of a relationship rather than some antiquated notion of an everlasting love."

Everlasting love? Of course he didn't want that. He didn't believe in it. Enough people who'd vowed to love each other forever paraded through his office every day. Of course he didn't believe in love. The fact that he'd tried to talk clients into giving their relationships another shot only meant that he believed in commitment. In honoring a contract.

"Antiquated notion of love?" Cassie replied.

"How many marriages last? Not many. People get the words *commitment* and *convenience* confused. As soon as their commitment—their love—loses its convenience, they end up in my office." They'd had this argument before, and Cooper had always thought his argument was sound and logical. But suddenly it sounded hollow to his ears.

"Some people say 'I do' and mean it. You just don't see them in your office."

"Ha." His *ha* lacked oomph and he tried to think of a valid point he could make more oomphy. "Look at you and Gene. You didn't even make it to the altar before you decided your everlasting love wasn't all that lasting."

"Listen, Gene and I aren't the issue. I'm not asking you to marry Paula, just take her out on a date."

"I said fine. Dating's easy. It's anything more serious that gets difficult. Maybe you and I should have tried *dating* rather than all the *kissing* and *talking* we've been doing. Dating your friend is bound to work out wonderfully if all she's interested in is superficial. I'll ask her to dinner at Waves tomorrow night."

"Great," Cassie said, sounding like her normal chipper self, although there was something not quite normal about her expression. "I'm sure she'll love it."

"What about walking Dudley tomorrow?" he asked. "I don't think this Paula will consider walking a drooling mastiff much of a date." He patted the puppy's head. "Sorry, Dud."

"I'm sure I can manage one night without you."

Yes, Cassie had made it abundantly clear that she could do without him, Cooper thought as they finished the walk in silence. She didn't need him at all.

And of course he was fine with that.

They were just *friends*. He was beginning to hate that word.

The next night, Cassie watched Cooper and Paula speed away in his Mustang. Yeah, Cooper would probably love dating vampire-nailed Paula. She should be elated to have her elbow-crazed neighbor off her hands.

And yet . . .

And yet, she was falling in love with the anti-love divorce lawyer. Why on earth had she fixed him up with Paula? Because loving Cooper was scary.

She's always imagined that loving someone would be easy.

Thinking she loved Gene had been easy. Like Cooper had said, it was convenient even.

Being friends with Cooper had been easy, simple even.

But love—it complicated things.

They had very different beliefs—Cassie believed in love, and Cooper didn't.

They had very different expectations—Cassie wanted an ever-after sort of marriage and a family, Cooper wanted . . .

What did Cooper want?

Not Cassie, that's for sure. Look at the way he snapped up the opportunity to date Paula. No, a man who thought their kisses meant something would have been insulted, not pleased when Cassie offered to fix him up.

She might be falling for Cooper, but there was no way Cooper was ever going to fall for her. No, lawyers who believed in contracts and pre-nups, never fell. They were always prepared and steady.

"He's not going to change, is he Dudley?"

The dog just wagged his tail and a slime goober dropped with a splat to the floor.

"He's probably having a great time with Paula, isn't he?"

Dudley sank to the floor with thud. Not much of a conversationalist. This was going to be her life, eating her meals with a nonconversing, sliming dog.

Right now Cooper and Paula were probably being served their drinks. They were laughing and getting to know each other. But the relationship wouldn't go anywhere. Paula and Cooper weren't right for each other.

Who was right for Paula? Paula was working as a receptionist at the station as she finished up her Business degree at Mercyhurst, with a minor in Accounting. Who did she know that might interest someone like that? Hardworking, goal-oriented . . .

Gene Gifford, that's who.

Mr. Why-waste-money-for-a-wedding. Mr. Spell-out-your-expectations. Mr. Marriage-is-a-contract.

Of course, Cooper said he believed in the same things.

But she had a feeling about Gene and Paula. She didn't have even the slightest niggle of a feeling about Cooper and Paula.

Oh, yes, Cassie had a match for Paula, and by default, one for Gene. And if she matched Gene with someone else, he'd stop obsessing about a relationship with her that wasn't ever going to happen, that never should have started in the first place.

Now, how on earth was she going to introduce Paula and Gene? She'd managed to introduce Leo and Fran on the sly. There was no reason she could do the same with Gene and Paula. And since Cooper had said he planned to take Paula to Waves, the setup shouldn't be all that hard to put in place.

"What do you think, Dudley? A certain white dress is appropriate for Waves, right?"

The puppy whined and Cassie decided to take it as his agreement.

"I'm doing this for Gene and Paula's sake. I have a feeling that they could hit it off."

Dudley yipped.

"Honestly? Of course that's the honest reason."

Dudley's head plopped onto the linoleum and his jowls suctioned the slick surface making a *bluh, bluh, bluh* sound.

"Bluh, bluh, bluh? Why Dudley, I don't deserve that. You know I always put others first. If Paula and Gene hit it off and I'm stuck with Cooper, that's just a matter for fate to decide."

Dudley yipped.

"Okay, if I'm wearing the white dress I'll be driving Cooper nuts with elbows and maybe he'll forget about perky Paula's blood-red nails."

Another yip.

Cassie picked up the phone and dialed Gene's number. "Gene, it's Cassie. We have to talk."

Forty-five minutes later, Cassie tugged nervously at the hem of her dress. Maybe Cooper had been right, maybe it was too short.

"I'm so glad you've finally come to your senses," Gene murmured as they followed the maître d' to their table.

"Um, about that—"

"We're going to be so happy together, now that you've finally decided to be rational."

Cassie nodded as she scanned the restaurant for Cooper and Paula, but didn't see them. Maybe she and Gene had beat them to the restaurant. She hoped that was it. The alternative was that Paula and Cooper decided to go somewhere else. Then she'd be trapped having dinner with Gene for nothing.

The maître d' assisted her into her chair. "Your server will be with you momentarily."

"So, you wanted to talk? I knew you'd come to your senses eventually," Gene said with a superior smirk.

If Cassie hadn't already been convinced that Gene

Gifford was going down as her most dismal match-making mistake before, she would be now.

"Actually, I think you misunderstood my invitation. I didn't want to talk about us getting back together."

Gene's smirk faded in slow motion. "You don't?"

"No. I let my dreams of finding love, of building a life with someone blind me to the fact you and I will never suit. I wanted to love you, so I thought I did."

"But you don't."

"As a friend, Gene, you'll always be special to me. And that's why I asked you to dinner."

"To tell me I'll always be your special friend?" He didn't sound impressed with the designation.

"Well, yes, that, and that I have a feeling about a someone else for you. She's ambitious and working hard to better her life. And she's even studying for a minor in Accounting. The two of you would be perfect for each other."

"You're fixing me up?" He didn't look overly grateful.

"Gene, we'd never work out, but you and Paula have a lot in common. I'm just asking that you think about it."

"I'm sorry, Cassie. You see, this isn't what I expected and I'm not coping well."

"And you like to know what to expect."

"You know I do. That you live life on the edge of

chaos was something the bothered me. I thought I could teach you to be orderly."

She took a sip of her water and smiled. "No, I'm afraid I'm hopelessly fond of chaos."

"And of big dogs."

"Yeah, of Dudley too. And I'm fond of you as well, that's why we're here."

"Because you have a feeling about me and a particular woman," he said, still not sounding enthused.

"Right." She scanned the room again, hoping to see Cooper and Paula, but still came up with nada.

"Is she meeting us here?" Gene asked.

"In a manner of speaking."

His eyes narrowed suspiciously. "What manner?"

"You see, uh," Cassie tried to think of some way to explain her plan that didn't sound crazy. Unfortunately, she was pretty sure no matter how she put it, sounding crazy was a given. "Well, she doesn't really know about you yet."

"So she's coming here to meet you?"

Cassie shook her head. "Not to meet me. She's coming here on a date."

"With someone else?"

She nodded. That had gone better than she thought it would. "I'm afraid so."

"And you're going to tell her mid-date that she's got the wrong man?"

Maybe it hadn't gone so well. Gene's face looked decidedly flushed and his expression wasn't one of pleasure. "Well, I was thinking about something a bit more sneaky."

He sputtered for a few moments, then finally managed to spurt out just her name, "Cassie." He didn't need to say anything more for her to know he wasn't pleased with her grand scheme.

"I thought we'd invite Paula—that's her name, Paula—and her date to dine with us."

"Who's her date?" he asked.

She smiled, noting he hadn't said no. "Now, about her date. You see, that's the sticky part."

"The guy she's with is the sticky part? You mean the fact she doesn't know you're fixing her up with me and that we're about to shanghai her date isn't sticky?"

Cassie shrugged. "Okay, so maybe the whole thing is a bit sticky, but—"

"Who's she out with Cassie?" he repeated.

"Cooper."

Gene's eyes narrowed. "Your kissing neighbor?"

"One and the same."

"Why is he out with someone else if he's been kissing you?"

"Now, there's a long story involved with that answer. But it boils down to the fact that I'm a career woman, and he's a jaded lawyer. So I fixed him up."

"I don't understand."

"Well, we're all wrong for each other, but we still like kissing, and I think I'm falling in love with him, and that's just insane, so even though we've got Dudley together, and great chemistry, and a solid friendship, I still fixed him up because, I don't want to kiss him." That much was the truth. Cassie didn't want to kiss Cooper, didn't want to love a man who didn't believe in love, whose very profession was the antithesis to hers. No, she didn't want to . . . . "But I don't seem to be able to help myself. I think I love him."

Gene looked confused. "Cassie, over the course of our engagement, I grew accustomed to your odd way of thinking, but I'm afraid that last bit is too confusing for me to untangle."

"Hey, just imagine how I feel. Confused is just the tip of the iceberg. But all you need to do is meet Paula. I have a feeling that's all it's going to take."

"You know I really thought you and I had a future together, but I think the fact that you missed the wedding was the best thing that could have happened to us. I would have gone as crazy as you are if we were together."

"Gene, that's one of the nicest things you've ever said to me. I feel the same way. And could I give you a hint?"

"Sure," he said, shrugging and looking totally bemused. "Why not? You're obviously going to give it to me whether or not I want to hear it."

"When you and Paula decide to tie the knot you might want to consider something a bit more romantic than marrying around the schedule of a convention in order to save money."

"You've got better ideas?" he asked.

"Loads and loads. I'll give them to you anytime. I . . ." Her sentence died as she spied Cooper and Paula enter the restaurant. "They're here."

Cooper looked good enough to take Cassie's breath away. What was it about this man, this one man, that could make her good sense fly from the window as easily as looking at him could rob her of her breath?

He and Paula followed the maître d' through the crowded dining room, right toward Cassie and Gene's table. She knew the instant Cooper had spotted her. His smile faded and annoyance lit his face. "Cassie? What brings you out tonight?"

"Gene and I were just discussing—"

"Your wedding?"

"—our newly formed friendship. We might not have been meant to for marriage, at least not to each other, but that doesn't mean we can't be friends."

"Would you like to join us?" Gene asked.

"Please do," she said, shooting Gene a pleased look. "We're done with our talk and everything's okay between us now, right Gene?"

"Oh, everything is perfectly wonderful."

There was no escaping Gene's sarcasm, though Cassie hoped no one else noticed. One studied glance from Cooper assured her that he hadn't missed it.

Paula, who until now had been silent, gently tugged on Cooper's arm. "We'd better not. Cooper and I were going to take tonight to get to *know* each other."

"We have all night," Cooper said. "This will be fun, sharing a meal with *friends*."

Both Gene and Cassie grimaced at the word *friends*. Gene didn't want to be just friends with Cassie, though she was sure he'd change his mind when he fell head over heels for Paula. But then there was Cassie's friendship with Cooper. Watching him ease Paula's chair up to the table sent a wave of jealously flooding through her system. No, she didn't want to be Cooper's friend, despite what she kept telling him—and telling herself.

She wanted him to love her.

"So, you and good old Gene are all squared away?" Cooper, seated next to Cassie, asked conversationally.

"We're fine."

"You and Gene had a problem?" Paula paused a moment and then to Gene said, "I'm Paula, by the way."

"Paula. Nice to meet you," Gene said, shaking her hand, and holding it a split second longer than necessary.

"You had a problem with Cassie?"

"She stood me up."

"Gene . . . Gene . . . your name does sound familiar," Paula said.

"She didn't exactly stand good old Gene up for a date, did you Cassie?" Cooper smiled, but there was no warmth behind it. Cold, hard fury radiated like some wayward aura.

"The wedding."

"You're that Gene?" Paula asked.

"Yes," Gene said, looking pained.

"I'm so sorry," Paula cooed, reaching over and patting his hand. "To be stood up at your own wedding . . ."

She shook her head and tsked sympathetically. "Shame on you, Cassie."

"I was stuck in Florida," Cassie said, feeling the need to defend herself.

"I can see why you two are over. I'd never do that to someone I loved," Paula said. "I'd insist the airline get me there on time."

"That's what I suggested Cassie do," Gene assured her, looking much less wounded.

"Well, it's good that you're just friends now. You need something more in a woman." Paula had stopped patting his hand and now had her red-nailed talons resting on it.

"Yes, it's good you're friends," Cooper said. "I mean, Cassie's got lots of friends."

"Do you have something on your mind, Cooper?" Cassie asked. "Spit it out."

"The only thing on my mind is dinner. Where's our waiter?"

Paula stared at them for a minute, obviously aware of the subtle nuances between Cassie and Cooper, but unsure what they meant. Finally, trying for a safer topic, she asked, "So, what do you do, Gene?"

Moments later they were chatting amicably about contracts and accounts.

"So, what's your game now?" Cooper hissed at Cassie.

"I don't know what you mean."

"Yes, you do. And I want some answers. First you're kissing me, then you're running. Next thing I know you're flattened against me in your backyard, then you run again. We decide to be friends, you set me up on a date and then tail me with some lame excuse about making up with your ex-fiancé."

"You see—" Cassie stopped, suddenly aware Paula and Gene were hanging on their every word.

"You kissed Cooper and then fixed me up with him?" Paula asked.

"You asked me to," Cassie said, even though it sounded like a lame defense.

"But you didn't mention you'd been kissing him."

"You didn't ask. And I didn't want to be kissing Cooper."

"And then you show up here to break up our date," Paula continued.

"Not exactly. You see, I made a mistake."

"You mean you want to kiss me now?" Cooper asked.

"No. Yes. I mean, what I'm saying is, Paula, that while Cooper was a fine date for an evening, I simply set you up with him because you asked me to. Afterward, I had a feeling—"

"A feeling?"

"She gets these feelings about couples," Gene said. "I've told her over and over that relationships need to be based on more than just feelings. Mutual interests, and goals. A marriage is a contract between two people."

"You're so right." Paula nodded. "So many people go into relationships with rose-colored glasses and seem surprised to find out that eventually those glasses slip."

Cassie half expected Cooper to chime in with his agreement, but he remained silent on the subject.

Paula turned to Cassie. "So you had a feeling about me and someone other than Cooper?"

"Yes, Gene."

"Gene?"

"You and Gene. I have a feeling you'll both hit it off just fine."

"So, you want me to drop Cooper here, and go out with Gene."

Cassie was relieved it was out in the open. "I think that would be wise."

"What do you think, Gene?" Paula asked.

"I think I'd like to have a chance to get to know you." He smiled at her, and Cassie knew in her gut that these two were meant to be together. She knew that no matter what they said about being logical about relationships, this would be a happily ever after love match.

She'd helped figure out Gene and Paula's relationship.

Now if she could just figure out what to do about Cooper.

Cooper had given up trying to figure out his crazy neighbor, just as he'd given up trying to figure out the emotional roller coaster she seemed to cause him.

"So here we are again." They were parked in his driveway. Gene and Paula had driven off together. He had to admit, he was relieved. But now, sitting here with Cassie, he didn't know what to do.

"This seems to be a new trend. You and me, left behind while our dates go out together. Although, I'll confess, those two were made for each other. All that talk about contracts and numbers and . . . well, my *feelings* tend to agree with you. They'll make a perfect, albeit slightly boring, couple."

"Yes, they will." Cassie sounded genuinely pleased for both Gene and Paula. "I'm sorry I interrupted your date with Paula."

"Are you really?" he asked, his voice low.

She inched a bit farther away from him, although there wasn't much space to get away.

"Of course I am. Why would you think I wouldn't be?"

"It seems fixing me up and then breaking me up has become a new hobby for you, Cassie."

"The first time was your fault. You fixed me and Leo up."

"And this time?" he asked. "You still haven't given me a good answer as to why you set me and Paula up in the first place."

"Because she wanted—"

"She might have wanted, but I've seen you talk people out of things before. So, why didn't you convince her I wasn't right for her."

"I tried, but she didn't listen. I mean, by the time I was done talking about you she thought you were unemployed and starving in genteel poverty."

"You lied to her?" He chuckled.

"No. I just used that lovely lawyer trick of misdirecting people. Giving them just enough truthful information to form a totally wrong idea. It's a game I learned from you."

"Oh?"

"Cooper, I don't want to play games anymore."

"That's good because I was never very good at games. So, if we're no longer playing games, tell me what you want to do."

"Kissing comes to mind."

"I thought we were done with kissing."

"We've both been back and forth on this. We've analyzed it. Talked it to death. But no amount of talking or analyzing is going to change the fact that I can't seem to stop thinking about kissing you, about . . ."

"About what, Cassie?"

"About having something more than friendship with you," she blurted out in a rush.

"That's funny because something more than friendship seems to be on my mind an awful lot lately too. But—"

"Uh, oh. I hate it when you give that lawyerly *but*."

"But, I want to be clear here, Cassie. Over these last few months that I've gotten to know you, I've learned how you feel about relationships. They're all covered in pretty words like *love,* and *until death do us part.* This is an area you and I couldn't be farther apart on. I want you. I like you. We're friends and I think that's a wonderful place from which to build a relationship that's something more than friendship. I care for you. But I don't know if any of those things will be enough for you."

"I want it all," she admitted softly. "The pretty words, the feelings. I want those rose-colored glasses. I think I'm falling in love with you, Cooper. I love being friends with you, but it's grown to be so much more than that, and no matter how I try, I don't know how to go back to platonic friendship with you, and don't know that I'd want to. Loving you isn't easy, but it's there. Big. And growing bigger. But my loving you isn't enough. I want you to love me, too." Instead of backing away, she inched closer to him and softly laid her hand on his arm.

She was waiting for a reply. Not just any reply. She was waiting for him to say he loved her too. To paint her pretty word pictures. But Cooper couldn't bring himself to lie. "You see, that's the one thing I don't know if I can give you, Cassie. To be honest, I don't really believe that the kind of love you're talking about exists."

"I'm sorry you feel that way," she said softly. "And sorry that I broke up your date with Paula."

"Cassie, I don't want to hurt you." He was desperate to make her understand. "Really, I'm sorry."

"Better be clear now than later," she said softly.

"Just because I don't have all those poetic notions you do, doesn't mean we can't work. We're friends, Cassie. We're compatible. Or at least we were until you broke up with Gene. Friendship like that means something. We could make it more. Build a strong foundation for a relationship."

"A strong foundation doesn't mean anything without love. I'm sorry. Good night, Cooper." She reached out and gently touched his cheek. They'd said they were done before, but this time, there was a sense of finality in her voice. It scared him to death.

"But—"

The door slammed.

He sat in the car and watched her walk across the drive to her house, open the door and go in, leaving him all alone.

He imagined Dudley was excited to see her home. She probably was letting the puppy out back.

And he was out here, alone.

He should feel relieved. They'd danced around this attraction since she got home from her aborted wedding. Coming closer, pulling back, only to come closer once again. But this time, as the door slammed it signaled a sense of finality.

It, whatever *it* was that had been growing between them, was over for good.

Yes, he should feel relieved. But for some reason, he didn't.

Chapter Nine

"*Tonight's topic is change. I want to talk about being the type of person who's able to change their point of view and learn to look at life from a different perspective. More than just looking, the ability to change the course of your life. For instance, once I thought I was destined to marry and live happily ever after. Since my canceled wedding, I've changed my point of view and decided to dedicate myself to my job, and my dog. It's not what I had planned for my life, but I'm sure that I'm on the right course. If you've changed your life goals, call me. For myself, I guess some people are meant to help others find love, and that has to be enough . . .*"

The next day, Cooper couldn't get that sad look Cassie had given him off his mind. Sad and disappointed.

He could have pretended he could give her what she wanted, flowery prose and romance. But he was too honest for that.

Even though he knew this final break was for the best, there was an odd sort of hollow feeling in his chest. As if he'd lost something.

There was a knock on his office door. "Come in."

A man walked into the office. "Mr. Cooper? I'm Jason Granger."

Cooper forced Cassie's image out of his mind, and stood up to shake hands with his newest client.

His life was back in order. New clients, and eventually, new women.

"Take a seat, Mr. Granger." He gestured to the chair across from his. "Let's start with you telling me about your situation."

The thinning, gray-haired man sat and sighed. For a moment, he didn't say anything. Cooper was about to prompt him, when he finally said, "My wife and I are getting a divorce, and I heard you're the best."

"I don't know about that, but I do my best." He gave his routine, trust-me-I-can-get-you-through-this smile.

"And that's just what I'll need. She's going to try to take me to the cleaners, despite our pre-nup."

"Why is she out for blood, Mr. Granger? Another

woman?" That was the usual answer. Despite the fact he'd represented men who'd cheated in the past, Cooper felt a wave of distaste.

"Another woman?" Granger repeated. "Are you crazy? I can't even handle the one I had. Listen, my wife's insane. I didn't realize it until after we were married. She was demanding, freaked out every time I was late and didn't call, claimed she was worried about me, but I know it was just her way of controlling me, just like she tried to control everything about our relationship. She wanted the bed made, had a conniption if I didn't pick up after myself, and spent our anniversary crying and giving me those puppy-dog eyes of hers."

"Why did she cry on your anniversary?" Cooper asked.

"I forgot it, but I told her I'd make it up to her. Made reservations at a five star restaurant, sent her flowers, even had my secretary run over to the jewelers for a trinket. Still, you'd have thought I'd kicked a dog, rather than just forgotten a day."

Cooper knew he wasn't the most romantic guy in the world, but even he would have realized that sending a secretary out to buy a *trinket* for an apology wouldn't work. "Why do you suppose the day meant so much to her?"

"Because, like I said, she's crazy . . . sentimental. Do you know she has to watch that Rudolph special every Christmas?" His voice softened, and he had an almost wistful expression. "I mean, Rudolph? That's for kids. But she's like that. I offered to buy her the DVD, but she said no, she had to watch it on network television because that's what her family does every holiday, watch it together."

"Did you ever watch it with her?" Cooper asked.

"No. I mean, do I look like the kind of guy to waste and evening on a kid show?"

"Maybe if you were sharing the evening with her, doing something that was obviously important to her, it wouldn't be a waste."

"Are you a marriage counselor, or a lawyer? I came here for an attorney, not for more touchy-feely crap."

Cooper tried to fight his Cassie-isms. But they just kept coming out. He could sense another potential client was about to walk out of his office.

He could *feel* that this man still loved his wife.

Cassie and her feelings had infected him like some kind of virus. But he couldn't seem to stop himself as he answered Mr. Granger, "I'm a lawyer, not a psychiatrist, Mr. Granger. But before I take your case, I want to be sure this is what you want. And sitting here across from you, I'm not sure it is."

"No, it's not what I want. She left me, after all."

"Why do you imagine she did that?" Cooper asked.

"For all the reasons we just talked about. I'm a workaholic, according to her. She wants more than I can give her."

"Can or will?"

"What?" the man asked.

"She wants more than you *can* give, or *will* give?"

"It's the same thing."

"I don't think so. There's a big difference."

"But . . ." The man sat a moment, obviously lost in thought, then he focused back in and shook his head. "It doesn't matter. She wants out. She wouldn't be interested in giving it another try, about what I can, or would give to have her back."

"You don't know that if you don't talk to her."

"I wouldn't know what to say."

"Why did you marry her?" Cooper asked.

"Because I love her. I mean, she's sentimental and crazy, but I love her."

"*Love* her, not *loved* her. I think that's a telling statement."

"There you go, playing shrink again," Granger said, not sounding very disgruntled.

Cooper knew the man was wrong. He wasn't playing shrink. No, he was pretending to be a disc jockey who might say she was done with romance, but had the most sentimental, romantic heart of anyone he'd ever met.

"So, you think I should . . ." Granger let the sentence trail off.

"Talk to her. Tell her you love her, and that you'll try to change."

"I don't know if I can."

"And you'll never know if you don't try. Try going for walks, and ice cream. Women love ice cream. Maybe buy her a dog."

"A dog?" Granger was looking at Cooper as if he was the one who was insane.

"Something big and not so bright. And maybe buy her that DVD of the Rudolph holiday special and show up with that, saying you want to make up for not watching it last year. That you'd like to be around to watch it on network this year. And bring her an anniversary card. It would be late, but still, women care more about the thought than anything. Offer to make every day an anniversary and Christmas if she'll give you another try."

"That's totally sappy," Granger said, looking perplexed.

Cooper nodded happily. "Women like sappy and they like grand gestures, something to let them know you care."

Granger stood, shaking his head. "You're the oddest freakin' divorce lawyer I've ever met."

"Yeah, I know," Cooper said with a sigh. It was all Cassie's fault. "You have my number if it doesn't work, but I have a feeling you won't be needing it."

The man paused a moment, then stuck out his hand and shook Cooper's. "Thanks."

"You're welcome. Let me know how it turns out, one way or another."

Granger nodded, then walked out of the office.

Cooper realized Cassie had rubbed off on him more than he knew. He'd sounded just like her on her radio show as he tried to convince his potential client that love was worth it. He'd done it because he'd seen something in the man's eyes when he said he wanted a divorce. Something like pain. And he'd known that the man loved his wife, that it was more than just compatibility.

He had a *feeling* he knew just what it was . . .

Love.

He thought about Cassie. He did believe they could be compatible and build a strong relationship. But it was more than that.

He needed her.

He wanted her.

It went deeper still.

He loved her.

Truly, loved her.

He loved that she continually lost her keys. Loved that she wanted nothing but happiness for everyone who surrounded her, both at work and in her personal life. He loved that she had the sexiest elbows he'd ever seen. He loved her laugh, her smile, her giant heart and he even loved her giant, slimy dog.

He loved who he'd become since he met her. He thought about Granger and hoped he worked it out with his wife.

Maybe he couldn't save every couple's marriage, but maybe he could save a few. He realized his beliefs on marriage had changed because of Cassie. He believed a marriage was more than just a contract that could be broken. It was important and worth working at before calling it quits.

Cassie had given him that as well.

And suddenly, Cooper knew just how much he wanted to give her in return. The trick was going to be convincing her to let him.

Chapter Ten

"*Hi, this is Night Calls here at WLVH, where love is more than just a song.*"

"*Hi, Cassie. I'm faxing you a letter right now, hoping you'll pick me as your Splash Bash date.*"

"*Thank you, caller. I'll make sure I watch for it. Is there anything in it that would set you apart from the other men who've entered the contest?*"

"*Well, I'm not rich, or gorgeous, though people don't tend to shriek when they see me on the street. I live in a quiet eastside neighborhood, nothing pretentious, just homey. I knew the minute I saw the house that it was meant for me. Or maybe, to be more exact, I knew the minute I saw the woman who would be my neighbor, that it was the perfect house for me.*"

172

"Your future neighbor?"

"I didn't know it at the time, but she would become one of my best friends. Oh, we are polar opposites. She has this happily ever after view of relationships, and I am a bit more jaded. You see, I'm a divorce lawyer. I know from experience that a lot of marriages don't end with her happily-ever-afters. But she's taught me that some marriages do."

"You believe that some relationships are more than just convenience?"

"Yes. You see, what it comes down to is the person you're with. It requires work, patience, but more than any of that, it requires a whole lot of love."

"I see. And you put all of this into your letter? That's why I should pick you?"

"You should pick me because I've learned a lot from my neighbor, it just took me some time to admit how much. As a matter of fact, I've lost clients because of her. Just had another walk out of my office this afternoon."

"Why's that?"

"Because they come in to hire me to represent them in a divorce, and I start talking them out of it, reminding them that love is work and that they should give it another chance."

"You didn't."

"Guilty as charged. My neighbor's changed me, and I'd like to try and show you the changes. So, go

find my fax, and Cassie, I hope you pick me for your Splash Bash . . . and maybe more."

Cassie sat with Craig, both with a pile of letters in front of them.

"There's no way to pick one," Craig moaned for the umpteenth time.

"I said I liked that Melody who called in. She felt like a good match for you."

"You and your feelings about people."

"You can try to intellectualize what happens between two people, you can talk about compatibility, about intellectual connections, but when it comes down to it, all you can really trust are your feelings."

"If that's the case, why are you even bothering to look through your pile." He took her pile of letters and slid it away from her. "You know who your heart's telling you to choose."

"What are you talking about?"

"Cassie, I'm not just your boss, I'm your friend. And I know that from the moment Jonathan Cooper moved in next door to you, nothing's been the same. I also listen to your show, and I know his letter's in this pile somewhere." He patted the papers. "I know it's the one you want to pick, that he's the only man you want to go to the party with."

"But I've decided to be a career woman—"

"You can be a career woman and still be in love."

Cassie didn't deny the feeling . . . she couldn't.

"But sometimes love's not enough," she said softly. "Especially when it's one-sided. I can believe in love all I want, but Cooper doesn't. He's too jaded by his job."

"I heard his call the other night. He's not a jaded man . . . at least not anymore. He loves you, Cassie. And anyone who's heard you talk about him, or seen you with him, would have to be crazy not to know how you feel about him. Don't let fear keep you from following your heart."

"I—"

"Pick his letter, Cassie."

"I haven't read it yet."

"Why?" he asked.

"Because I'm afraid. Really, down-to-the-bones afraid. I thought I loved Gene, but in the end, I just loved the idea of being in love. And now, such a short time later, I think I'm in love with Cooper? What if I'm wrong? And maybe Cooper thinks he's changed, but . . ." She let the sentence die there because she didn't know what to say.

"Cassie, let me have his fax."

She wanted to say no, but found herself digging through her pile to the sheet of paper she knew was Cooper's. It was folded in half and looking definitely worse for wear. She'd folded it, toyed with it, used it as a coffee mat. She'd stuffed it in her pocket, in her purse, in her desk drawer.

Craig opened it, and within seconds, put it back down.

"Well," she said.

"Pick him."

"What if it's a mistake like Gene?"

Craig just smiled and shook his head. "Trust me, it's not."

She held out her hand, but Craig held onto the paper. "I'll give it to you later. For now, just trust me and pick him."

"And you?"

"Looks like I'm going to the Beach Bash with a woman named Melody."

Cassie looked up and down the beach, watching for Cooper. He'd called her house and said he'd be late.

Figures.

Normally being on Presque Isle soothed her. She loved the beach, loved the smells and the sound of the waves. But today she felt definitely less than soothed.

Cooper had stood her up.

Her mood picked up a bit when she caught sight of Craig and Melody. She seemed nice, and Cassie had a feeling that they just might hit it off.

"Cassie," Ted called. "We need you on the stage."

Ted was positively beaming. The crowd was as large, if not larger, than last year's. He was feeling smug. Little did he know that Craig was helping her plot a surprise holiday contest featuring Ted as the prize.

"Cassie," he called again.

She smiled at him, thinking about her Christmas revenge.

"Sure, Ted," she said cheerily.

He eyed her suspiciously, and for a moment she thought he was going to ask her a question, but he simply shrugged and walked toward the makeshift stage.

Cassie's smile faded as she took one last look around. Maybe Cooper had changed his mind. Reluctantly, she walked onto the stage.

"Hello, Erie!" she called, trying to fake enthusiasm she didn't have. "Welcome to WLVH's second annual Splash Bash. Let's start by giving a hand to our station manager Craig and his contest date, Melody."

The crowd burst into applause.

Cassie smiled. "Yes, the Win-a-Date Contest was a fifty percent success. It looks like my date stood me up."

The crowd booed and a couple voice could be heard offering to fill in.

"Thanks, but don't worry about it. I've had enough man-related trauma this year. It's probably a good thing he didn't show up. And after all, who needs him when I've got all of you? So, let's take the summer season out with a bang and start our afternoon off with a big Happy Anniversary to WLVH's morning duo, Punch and Judy, whose marriage at our first annual Splash Bash helped prove that our saying, WLVH, where love is more than just a song, is accurate! Punch and Judy, come on out."

The morning DJ couple rushed onto the stage to the sounds of applause from the audience. Cassie moved back onto the sand and clapped her hands along with everyone else.

The two of them looked so happy. She remembered how tense their courtship had been, and how it obviously had been worth it.

She sniffed, willing herself not to cry. Because, really, there was nothing to cry about. She'd decided to be a career woman.

"Well, here we are, Judy. Our anniversary party is a huge success," Punch, AKA Peter O'Brien said. "You can't say I didn't go all out."

Judy Bentley O'Brien just laughed. "Oh, no you don't. You're not getting out of getting me an anniversary present that easily."

"Now, Judy," he said, grinning, "would I try to do something like that?" He batted his eyes and the crowd roared with laughter.

"My husband, the comic." Judy's affection was there for everyone to see.

Cassie watched the two of them banter back and forth and tried to fight back her feeling of envy. She and Cooper certainly had the back and forth stuff right. He was back to avoiding her, it looked like.

". . . Cassie."

She heard Judy say her name and looked up.

"Cassie, they want you onstage," Ted hissed, nudging her back toward the stage.

She walked up to join her two colleagues.

"Where's that date of yours?" Peter asked.

"Like I said, he stood me up."

"I don't think so," Judy said, smiling as she pointed to the other side of the stage.

There was Cooper dressed in a tux, and Dudley wearing a bow tie. They walked center stage, and stood in front of her.

Peter handed Cooper the mike, then he and Judy backed off the stage.

Cooper's slow smile stole Cassie's breath. "Cassiopeia Grant, you've truly ruined me. Since meeting you I've learned to love ice cream, big dogs, and chaos. I've learned that love and marriage take work, and I've spent the last week ruining my practice, trying to get potential clients to give their relationships another try. I've learned that sometimes feelings make more sense than logic. Because logic would dictate that the two of us—a disc jockey who's built her career on love, and a divorce lawyer—wouldn't have a prayer in the world of making it as a couple. But my feelings say there's no other woman for me. I know you plan to be a career woman, but I'm wondering if you'd consider something more? A career woman and . . . well, I'm hoping you'll consider taking me on in a permanent sort of a capacity."

"Such as?"

"Marriage," Cooper said. He stepped forward. "And before you start thinking of all the reasons why we shouldn't, let me give you the one reason why we should. I love you."

The crowd roared its approval and Cassie felt as if she should roar hers as well. Instead she took the microphone and loudly, so she could be heard over the continued applause, she asked, "Was that a proposal?"

Cooper nodded, grinning.

"Well, I guess there's only one appropriate answer . . ."

She flung dropped the mike, flung herself into his arms and whispered, "Yes," in his ear.

She'd thought their kisses to date had been sizzling, but this one . . . this one was so much more. Because this one had more than chemistry to it, more than friendship—it had love.

Epilogue

"This is Ted Hyatt here. I know, I'm not a disc jockey you're accustomed to hearing on the airwaves. As a matter of fact, I'm no DJ at all, but my station manager, along with Cassie from Night Calls, forced me into this. I'm here with—"

"Amy Nyak. I won this radio spot with Ted. And the two of us are here for another WLVH wedding. Yes, this is a station that over the last two years has truly proven that for them, love is more than just a song."

Ted made a scoffing noise and said, "Just don't be getting any ideas about us, Amy. You won this radio spot with me, but nothing more. Not like our station manager, Craig, who's sitting in front with his new fiancée, Melody."

181

"Sh," Amy said. "Things are getting ready to begin. Here come Mary and Ethan, WLVH's first couple from its Pickup Lines contest. Ethan looks quite fetching in his tux, and Mary—"

"Well, guys, let me just say too bad this is radio and not TV, because Mary's hot. And so is Judy, who's just walked in with her on-air and off-air partner, Punch."

"AKA Peter O'Brien. And ladies, I'm with Ted here in wishing you could see how hot Punch looks in his tux. But they're not the reason we're here today. There's Jonathan Cooper standing at the front of the church. Ethan and Peter have joined him, and the rest of his wedding party, while the women are on the other side of the altar, waiting for—"

"Here she is," Ted interrupted. "Cassiopeia Grant. Our Cassie makes a lovely bride as she walks toward the groom."

"Ted, is that a tear I see in your eye?"

He made a scoffing sound that the audience could hear.

Amy's soft laughter soon overrode it. "Yes, Ted's turned into quite the softy, but who could blame him. After all, he works at a station built around the idea that love is real. Now, the bride and groom have joined hands and begun their vows. Yes, it's another beautiful wedding for WLVH, where love is definitely more than just a song . . ."

DATE DUE